Ca$h

SHORTY

GOT

A

THUG

BY CA$H

ACKNOWLEDGEMENTS

Here comes the toughest part of writing the book. A thousand shout outs can't earn a single friendship. Because true friends aren't that shallow. But one slip of the mind, where I forget to mention someone can earn a staunch enemy. That's crazy. So let's do it like this: I would like to thank everyone from A to Z!

Check for me on Facebook: CashStreetlit-Author or email @ wcp.cash2@gmail.com

<u>DEDICATION</u>

This book is dedicated to every single person who support my literary career and continue to pray for my release. Thank you for your prayers. We'll try again in 2014. In the meantime, I will keep my head up and continue to bang out street classics.

One, <u>Ca$h</u>

PROLOGUE
<u>Niesha</u>

Have you ever loved anyone or anything so damn much that you risked your life to hold on to them or it? I'm talking about the type of love that gets deep down into your soul and won't allow you to think straight or to move on; the kind of love that can lift you up real high or drag you down so low.

Brazen, the man I love with every dang fiber in my body, is a nigga who loves the streets and the hustle so much that he can't let go. Not even when the game does him dirty.

Me, I'm Niesha, Brazen's wifey. And my dumb ass is so gone over that man I swear I must be blinded by his swag! Even when he lies to me and breaks my heart I don't let him go. Sometimes common sense tells me to walk away from his ass and never look back, but my legs won't move. It's like Brazen has me under a spell and it's much more than being dickmatized.

See, in spite of all the ups and downs, I know Brazen loves me. That is why I'm still with him hoping like a fool that I'll be able to get him out of the streets before the game takes us both under. Only time will tell, right?

Ca$h

Well here's our story . . .

CHAPTER 1

BRAZEN

I'm only two days home from doing a three year prison bid and already I'm dying to get my hustle on. Pumpin' drugs ain't the only thing a nigga can do but it's the life that I love. That's something Niesha can't seem to understand. A nigga gon' do what he do.

"Brazen, I'ma wait for you faithfully—*again,*" she emphasized while I was locked up for the third time since we've been together. "But, boy if you come home on the same BS that put you behind bars I swear on my unborn children that I will walk away from you and never look back. I am so tired of making these long drives to see you and having to go through all of the hassles. For real, Brazen, this doesn't make any kind of sense!" She would complain.

While on lock I would sit there in visitation and listen to wifey vent then I'd place her hands on mine, stare deep into her eyes and say something like, "I know baby. And you're one hunnid percent right—this shit is for the birds. I'ma walk straight when I get out this time because I'm tired of taking you through the ups and downs.

I would utter those words with so much sincerity that I almost believed them myself. But deep down I knew that I was not done with the game. The streets owed me too much to fold my hand without collecting the pot. I would just have to be wiser about how I made my moves.

Ni is just gonna have to let a nigga do what he do, nah mean? 'Cause I love the streets and the fast money as much as I love her sexy black ass.

Yo, here comes my baby now, just coming in from work looking all tasty in her hospital scrubs. Damn, shorty sexy as a muthafucka. Watch how I put it down.

CHAPTER 2

NIESHA

I'm driving home from my job at Atlanta Medical Center where I am a LPN. It's hot as an oven outside and the AC in my cute little Nissan Altima is acting up. But nothing can wipe the smile from my face now that my boo is home.

Brazen has been in and out of prison for the past ten years! I swear if he slips up again and goes back, I am not holding him down through another bid. "No way! Not happening!" I promise myself for what seems like the hundredth time.

We've been together since high school, and to this day Brazen is the only man I've ever been intimate with so it's very hard for me to let him go. But I swear I am not putting up with anymore of his mess. Anyway, I'm not even going to go there. I'm going to give my boo the benefit of the doubt and try not to think negatively.

Ca$h

I'm listening to Keyshia Cole's *The Way It Is* feeling all giddy inside because I am about to go home and get some of that good loving that makes me so dang crazy in love. After three long years of nothing but my finger and a toy, a chick is trying to overdose on some real dick.

I walk into the house hoping Brazen will have my bath water ready and be anxious to love me down. After all, we've been sex-ting back and forth all day sending each other erotic text messages that has my kitty-kat purring.

I climb out of the car and hurry up the stairs on legs that can't wait to get hoisted up on my man's shoulders. I expect Brazen to push me up against the wall and devour me the second I step in the door. Instead I get, "Ni, my nigga Juvie 'bout to come through and scoop me up. I'ma be back in a couple hours."

Brazen says this shit to me out of his mouth without offering me as much as a peck on the lips. Add to that, this negro promised me that once he touched down he would not commence to hanging out with his mans and them again. I'm so angry my lips quiver!

9

Shorty Got a Thug

"Brazen, you haven't been home a good forty-eight hours and already you're breaking promises," I stiffly remind him. Then I sling my Gucci bag down on the sofa showing my frustration.

"Nah shorty, it ain't even like dat. This nigga Juvie owes me," claims Brazen with a straight face that I want to slap him across.

"What—eva!"

He pulls me into his strong arms. At five-five my head is against his hard chest. Brazen stands at six-two and weighs a sculpted two-hundred and ten pounds. I feel his hard dick pressing against my body, causing my titties to perk up.

"What's the matter, Dark Cream?" asks Brazen, using the pet name he has for me.

"Nothing." I respond unconvincingly and with a pout.

I don't feel that it's wrong for me to expect all of my man's time, at least for the first week or two that he's home. Dang, don't a girl deserve something for giving him undying loyalty throughout his prison bids?

Ca$h

Brazen lifts my chin up and stares down into my watering eyes. "Talk to me Ni. You feelin' some kinda way?" he asks.

I can't hold back. I have given this man so much of me, I deserve his all in return. I've smuggled weed and cell phones inside my vagina to him in prison. Pawned my jewelry to get money to retain a lawyer for him and that's not the half of it.

A tear falls from my eye.

"Brazen, I didn't see Juvie and them driving up and down the highway to visit you every weekend for three years. Nor do I recall them sending you money for commissary every week." My words come out through sniffles but they seem to bounce off of Brazen without effect.

"Don't even go there, Ni." He brushes off my feelings. Still I continue on.

"Where was those niggas when you needed packages and all of that?" I ask with an aching heart.

Brazen licks his lips and let's out a sigh. I wrap my arms around his waist and plead, "Baby, I'm just asking you to consider my feelings. Does your friends mean—"

11

Shorty Got a Thug

The sound of a car horn outside my door cuts off my words. Brazen unwraps his arms from around me and says, "That's probably Juvie. I'ma talk to you when I get back."

He kisses me *this damn quick* and he's out the door.

CHAPTER 3

Brazen

As I walk out of the door I can feel Niesha's pain jabbing me in the back. I hear her sniffles but I don't turn around. It ain't that I don't care about wifey's feelings, but the streets are calling and I gotta answer.

I step out the door rockin crisp baggy Evisu jean shorts, a white t-shirt, and a fresh pair of Prada sneakers. My 'do is tight, displaying a sea of waves. I slide on a pair of dark Prada shades which cover my baby browns while the intense May sun kisses my copper brown skin.

Behind the dark shades I'm rockin, my eyes focus on the 2009 Chrysler 300 my nigga just stepped out of. That bitch is pearl black, sitting on thirty inch black rims. Young Jeezy's new joint OJ is blasting from the Bose system. Juvie is Gucci'd down to the feet and his jewels is hurting 'em. A thick platinum chain hangs around his neck down to an inch above his waist. A diamond encrusted lion's head medallion swings on the end of the chain. An icy watch blings from his left

13

wrist as a diamond and ruby bracelet adorns his right one. When he smiles I see that he's grilled out with thirty-two platinum teeth. With his long locks he resembles Lil Wayne.

Homey must be eating real good.

I instantly feel some kinda way. Because not one muthafuckin' time did Juvie send me a crumb while I was on lock. I wonder if this nigga forgot that I always showed him love.

"What it do, fam?" he asks.

We embrace like hood niggas do.

"I'm ready to get what the game owes me," I finally respond as I step back and digest my nigga's profile.

A Lyfe Jennings' song plays in my mind.

Rollin' in my two door Monte Carlo/Lookin' for somebody I can borrow/Five or ten dollars 'til tomorrow/I'm doin' bad ya'll, uh-uhn/I just smoked my last pack of cigarettes today/You ever seen a nigga diggin' in the ashtray/It's a crumblin' and humblin' sight to see/I'm doin' bad ya'll, ah-hah/And their teasin? Me with these twenty three's/And these

14

Ca$h

DVDs in their ride/And they pass me by, b-b-by,
b-b-by/And have the nerve to wonder why/I be
robbin' these niggas

Juvie correctly interprets the slight scowl on my
face. He says, "Yo what's with the mean mug, nigga?"
He throws his hands up like he's Floyd Mayweather Jr.
and playfully jabs me in the chest. His fist hit nothin'
but solid muscle.

"Dayum! You done got ya weight up, ain't ya?"
he grins and the sun bounces off his platinum grill.

"Yeah, a nigga was on those pushups real hard
in the pen. But fuck all that." I cut to the chase. "I see
you're out here stuntin' and everything. Why you ain't
send a nigga a grip or nothing? Man, you left the whole
burden on my girl and you claim to be my *brotha from
anotha?*"

My jaws twitch with the hot anger that betrayal
brings about. I'm heated because I've busted them thangs
many times in defense of this nigga standing in front of me.
Juvie ain't never been no killa so when killas would try to
get at him, I popped them thangs and turned nigga's white
tee's red.

15

Shorty Got a Thug

Juvie owed me some major fuckin' with.

He puts up a hand to stop the verbal venom he could tell that I was about to unleash on his shady ass. "Let's ride out, fam. I'ma explain things to you," he counters.

See, Juvie is the type of dude that thinks he can talk his way out of the jaws of a hungry lion. But ain't nothin' he can say that will justify the disloyalty he showed while I was on lock. For one thousand ninety-five consecutive days I sat in a cell plotting this nigga's death. A slick tongue can't protect him from the inevitable.

Out of pure curiosity to hear what sad song he will sing, I slide into the passenger seat of his whip and we mash out. A song by The Game is beating from the car's system. Juvie voice commands the system to lower the volume. Nigga is straight stuntin', tryna impress a muthafucka.

"Before we chop it up, I'ma swing by the mall and let you cop a wardrobe," offers Juvie.

"Nigga, I ain't no bitch! You don't placate me with no muthafuckin' trip to the mall!" I explode. My nose is flared and lines crease my forehead. I'm tempted to slap his ass for tryin' me like dat.

Juvie hand flies up in protest. "Calm down, fam. Man, I didn't even worry about you while you was on

16

lock. I knew you would hold your own on the inside and I knew Ni was gonna hold you down on everything else. So I concentrated on gettin' my dough up out here for you when you touched down," he says.

I grill him as I weigh his explanation.

"Now that you're home, I got you, nigga," he adds.

I look out the window at passing traffic and simmer down as I toss his words around in my head. He can tell that I'm fighting hard to control the beast within so he spits some more good shit to assuage me. I nod my head like it's all good but it's not.

We hit the mall and drop more than ten bands on gear. I cop all the latest shit, although wifey had already maxed out her credit cards on a wardrobe for me before I came home. But Juvie owes me so I accept the gesture as a peace offering.

We dip from the mall and hit the Ritz on Old National Highway. At the plush hotel I follow Juvie into a suite where I find two butt naked, dimed up honeys awaiting me. One is preening in the wall mirror. She's about five-seven, with a small waist and a large ass that's complimented by a small set of titties. Baby girl is light-skinned with auburn red hair that flows down her back.

"Helloooo." She speaks in a sort of sing-song voice and smiles sweetly at me.

"Sup, li'l mama." I speak back. Then I nod at the other cutie who is sitting on the bed in nothing but a red thong and bra.

"What's poppin', Miss Lady?"

"Any and everything," she replies demurely, licking her lips that are heavily glossed.

"I'm talking ménage." I smirk.

"We wouldn't have it any other way," she says and her girl nods in agreement.

"Im'a bounce. Ya'll welcome my nigga home," Juvie instructs the two hotties.

"We certainly will," promises shorty on the bed.

I walk my nigga to the door and whisper, "You got some condoms, homie?"

"I never leave home without 'em." He pulls a couple of rubbers from the pocket of his Red Monkey jeans and hands them to me. "Don't hurt yaself." The smirk on his face causes me to laugh.

Ca$h

"Nigga, I'ma have both of those hoes walking gapped legged by the time you get back," I boast.

I close the door behind Juvie and turn to look at the double fun that awaits me. Ni comes to mind in a brief moment of guilt which I quickly push aside.

What Ni don't know won't hurt her.

A man is gonna be a man.

CHAPTER 4
NIESHA

I cannot believe this shit. Brazen left home at 6 p.m. and it is now three o'clock in the damn morning and he hasn't called or returned. I swear, I am not going through this crap again with him. I have been down this road way too many times.

I know he's somewhere with his boy sniffing behind some trifling bitch. Because that's how Juvie gets down; he's a whore who tries to run up in everything with a skirt wrapped around it. Juvie's cruddy ass even had the nerve to try to step to me. Of course I would never tell Brazen or it would lead to a homicide.

Anyway, I can't blame Juvie for anything Brazen does. Brazen is very much his own man. However, I do blow up Juvie's phone trying to track down Brazen. But I repeatedly get sent to voicemail.

Now I'm hot!

Forget crying like some prissy chick, this is about to make me act real ghetto. As soon as Brazen walks in that door I'ma catch an assault case on his black ass. I did not

Ca$h

sacrifice things I needed to send him commissary money, make weekend trips to see him, and pay astronomical phone bills for his collect calls for him to get out of prison and do me like this.

Ooh, wait! I hear a car pull up in the driveway. I speed dial my cousin Carmen, awakening her from her sleep. Hello, she answers groggily.

"Cuz, wake up! It's me—Ni!"

"Ni? What time is it?" She yawns.

"Three fifteen."

"In the a.m.?" she asks in a high pitch.

"Yes!"

"Wow, gurl what's wrong?" she asks.

"Be on standby, I think I'm going to need bail money!"

CHAPTER 5

Brazen

I look at the Rolex on my wrist. It's an icy piece that Ni bought me when she inherited fifty stacks after her grandmother passed away four years ago. The watch is like new since I got locked up a few months after I got it and never got the chance to floss it much.

It's a quarter to three in the morning, dayum! Straight up, when I left with Juvie earlier today I had no intentions of creepin' on my girl. But when I fell up in that hotel suite and saw all that ass, pussy and titties, a nigga couldn't refuse it. Then time just flew by.

Juvie returned about midnight to scoop me up but I was balls deep in pussy for the third time this evening so leaving wasn't an option. Hell yeah I know I'm dead ass wrong for staying out so late without at least hittin' Ni up and telling her something. "Now it is what it is, so fuck it," I tell Juvie as we bounce from the Ritz.

Ca$h

"Wifey ain't gon' slap you around for staying out this late is she?" jokes Juvie as we roll up in my driveway.

I look over in the driver's seat at him like he's just disrespected my gangsta. "Fam, Ni don't run shit but her mouth. Anyway I'ma fuck with you tomorrow, dawg. Good looking out on the gear and those freak hoes."

"Anytime fam. I fucks wit'chu the long way. Now that you're back on the scene we can really get that check out here. Niggas ain't gon' be able to fuck wit' us." He smiles.

"That's what it is then." I pound my man, gather up the bags of gear and head inside the crib.

As soon as I step through the door I'm greeted with a hard slap across the face.

"Yo baby, what the fuck?" I stammer.

Ni's response is a two piece to my face. The punches land in quick succession. "I'm not your baby apparently nigga!" She spews as tears streak down her face and she pummels me with a flurry of punches.

I block most of the blows, duck a wicked backhand then I grab her arms and pin them to her sides. "Shorty, chill out!" I grit.

Shorty Got a Thug

"Let go of me, Brazen!" she yells, kicking and fighting.

I try kissing her to calm her down. But why in the hell did I do that? Ni goes snap! "Don't put your nasty ass lips on me. Go back to wherever you've been all night!" She snatches herself out of my arms and shoves me off of her.

"Baby, will you calm down and listen," I plead.

Wifey is not tryna hear it. She looks at me with a look that could push a nigga's scalp back. "I'm telling you, Brazen, if you don't get your shit and leave one of us is going to the morgue this morning and the other to jail. Trust, I'm too cute to be in anybody's morgue so I have my bail money on standby."

"So what you saying?" I ask, looking bewildered.

"Negro, did I stutter?" Her nose is turned up at me and she's gritting her teeth.

"Why you buggin', Dark Cream?"

"Do not call me that! I cringe every time that name comes out your mouth because it's always followed by a lie or some other type of deception. *I'm not your baby. I'm not your Dark Cream. And I'm not your woman.* Take your ass back to the bitch you just hopped out of bed with."

24

Ca$h

"Shorty, you got the game fucked up, I would never play you like that. Damn. Why you always accusing me of the next bitch? When you do that shit, it makes me wanna go out there and do it since you think I'm doing it anyway," I counter, to hide my guilt.

"How dare you come at me like that!" She huffs up as if she's ready to swing at me again. Her fist are balled up at her sides. "Brazen, how many times while you were on lock did you accuse me of things I would never do? Yet not once did I feel the urge to go out and do them and do you know why?"

I don't reply but I know the answer even before she verbalizes it.

"I didn't feel the urge, *Brazen* . . . because I love you, and I have too much respect for myself and for you to give the next man what belongs to *you*. See, I'm a faithful woman and I'm loyal. Two qualities that you don't seem to possess." She rails on me.

"So you think a nigga would cheat on you?"

"In a hot minute! And it's not like you haven't done it in the past."

Shorty Got a Thug

"Why you gotta keep bringing that up?" I ask, walking out of the living room and heading upstairs to take a shower with Ni on my heels.

In the bathroom I manage to calm her down. I swear to her that I have not been out creepin'. "That's on everything I love," I vow and she allows me to kiss her.

"You better not be lying," she mumbles as I suck on her tongue.

"I'm not, baby. Now run me some bath water." I encourage her with a pat on the ass.

Ni sits on the edge of the bath tub and turns on the water while I unzip my pants to take a piss. As soon as I pull out my joint, Ni snaps, "What the fuck?"

My eyes follow hers and I realize that I am busted. I'm still wearing a condom. Damn, I'm slippin'.

CHAPTER 6

NIESHA

It has been three weeks since I kicked Brazen out of my house and I have not spoken to him not once since then. I probably should be screaming *hurrah*! And dancing around the living room. But I'm not.

The pitiful truth is, I miss my boo like crazy. I can't eat or sleep and the stress has caused me to lose ten pounds that I did not have to spare. Now my ass has been reduced to a booty. I'm stressing and I need my man back. I'm tired of pretending to be hard. I might as well admit it, I can not do without that man! Like Xscape sang back in the day, *"Clap my hands, stomp my feet…Every little thing that he does to me . . . feels so good.*

Except the heartache. But I'm not thinking about that at this moment. Lately I've cried so much my irises look *red.*

I'm in my living room, on the sofa crying on Carmen's shoulder. "I want my man back."

Shorty Got a Thug

"Hmmph! I don't know why," she scoffs. "All that nigga ever does is let you down and break your heart, cheat on you, and go back and forth to jail. And did I mention that time he gave you a STD? Dumb ass!"

"Some comfort you are." I'm heavy on the sarcasm.

"Well, you need to hear the truth," she says while at the same time texting Desmond, one of her many male friends.

Maybe I do need to hear the raw truth about Brazen, but now is not the time. "You know what cuz? I've changed my mind. I don't need any comforting, I'll give myself a hug. Just let me cry alone."

I get up and show her to the door.

Carmen grabs her Louis Vuitton bag and tosses her hair back as she follows behind me saying, "Whatever Ni, but until you show Brazen that you can do just fine without his ass he's gonna continue to show his behind."

"Yep, you're right." I hurry her out the door.

As soon as she's gone I call Juvie.

"Sup?" he answers.

I hear women's voices in the background.

"Hi Juvie, this is Niesha. Have you seen Brazen today?"

"Hold up."

A few seconds later Brazen comes on the line.

28

Ca$h

"What?" Is how the mutha effer has the nerve to greet my call.

I take a deep breath and fight back the tears. "Is that how you greet wifey?" I ask with hurt feelings.

"Nah, but you're not wifey anymore, right?"

Brazen's tone is nonchalant like it doesn't matter one way or the other. I'm dying inside. Part of me wants to kill him for showing no appreciation for the ten years I've put up with his shit and never once violated his trust in me, and part of me wants to beg him to come back home and make up. You know, give me some of that love that makes me know he's mine. And yet it's not just the great sex that has me sprung. I recall the candle light dinners, the walks in the park, and other tender moments that we have shared.

"Brazen," I respond sincerely, "don't play with me. You know my heart belongs to you and only you. That's why you're always hurting me. You feel that you have me wrapped around your little finger."

Brazen's laugh helps to evaporate my anger. "So can a nigga come home?" he ask needlessly.

"Brazen, of course you can. But answer this first: who are the birds I hear chirping in the background?"

"Nobody."

29

Shorty Got a Thug

I want to challenge him but I'm afraid to start an argument that might lengthen our estrangement.

Sensing my suspicion Brazen explains, "Baby, those are just hood chicks that do some work for Juvie, and all three of 'em are busted up."

We both laugh.

"Anyway, I'm on my way home so we can make up— you know how we do so be waitin' with nothing on but those red knee high boots I like. And put on those red glasses that make you look like a librarian. I'ma bring the wine and plenty of dick." He entices me.

Just thinking about what's about to go down has my legs shaking. On a normal day Brazen's sex is ridiculously good, but absolutely nothing compares to our makeup sex. But what I crave and miss most of all is simply the comfort of him lying next to me.

"Hurry Brazen!" I beg. "My legs are shaking with anticipation."

CHAPTER 7

Brazen

"Fam, I'ma get at you later," I tell Juvie after I hang up from my girl.

"A'ight my dude. You going back to wifey, huh? You can't do without Ni, and she can't live without you," he jokes.

"Yeah, well that's my other half. Don't hate, bruh. Really, it's not a good look."

I gather up my gear and bounce amid protest from the birds who were supposed to be tonight's entertainment. All three of the girls are candy yams but neither of them are Ni so I push on.

Fa real, I'm missing shorty as much as I would miss my right arm if I lost it. I creep but that doesn't mean I don't love wifey. A nigga's dick ain't got no conscience. I climb up in the midnight blue Explorer that I copped the other day. Then I take out my cell phone and call Ni.

"Hello?" she answers.

"Hey shorty. Are you naked?"

Shorty Got a Thug

"Yes. I just got out the shower."

"Good. I can picture your body; the way your titties stand up and how firm they are. Your small waist and your wide hips. And that ass! See, that's that shit that will make me smash a muthafucka if you ever give it away."

"I won't Brazen—not ever."

"You bet' not. Now tell me, do you still have that pussy shaved with that cute little patch of hair over it?"

"Yes, Brazen. That's the way you like it so I haven't changed it."

"Damn right. Who you belong to?"

"Your crazy ass."

"Okay, just so you never forget it."

"How could I do that? I think about you twenty-four-seven."

"I know you do, baby girl. Now lay across the bed and rub your pussy for me. Rub it real slow and call out my name," I cooed.

"Umm—Brazen—Brazen—Brazen. My fingers are stroking my rose petals. Slowly—up—and—down." She purred.

"Spread those pretty lips and push your finger inside like it's my tongue."

I hear Niesha's breathing increase.

32

Ca$h

"Yeah, just like that baby," I urge. "Do that while I take my dick out and stroke this muthafucka."

"Oooh, Brazen, your voice is turning me on."

"Yours is turning me on too shorty. I'm already boned up."

"Oh my god. Is it real hard?"

"Like steel," I answer truthfully. I'm trying my best not to run off the road.

"Umm, I am sooo wet. You hear my pussy squishing? You have me so fucking hot. Tell me I'm your bitch."

I know Ni is hot as hell when she talks gutta like that.

"You're my bitch and my wifey too," I say as I steer the truck with one hand and stroke my dick with the other.

"Bra....zen?"

"Yes baby?"

"I'm rubbing my clit. It's sooo fuckin' hard. Daaammmmmnnn, it feels so good. Hurry your ass home, boy."

"I'm doing ninety in a sixty-give zone, shorty. I'll be there in a minute. Just close your eyes and think about the first time I ate your pussy."

Shorty Got a Thug

"Oh my god!"

"Your pussy tasted so good, and it still has me fucked up to this day."

"Brazen—damnnnnn— hurry up."

"I'm turning into our subdivision now."

I whip up in the driveway and pull up besides NI's whip, still getting that pipe nice and rocked up for her. I continue to phone sex her until I'm in the house, upstairs in the bedroom standing before her with a massive bone.

The bedside lamp is dimmed. I rub the huge head of my dick across Ni's lips as I drop my cell phone on the floor and step out of my jeans. "What you wanna do with this big, black pussy punisher?" I ask arrogantly.

"Treat it like a Snickers bar." She smiles as she reaches out and wraps two hands around it.

Ni licks the head then opens her mouth wide to accommodate my girth. I close my eyes and see paradise.

CHAPTER 8

Niesha

"Umm, daddy, your dick taste so damn good in my mouth," I mumble as I slurp on the bulbous head. His thickness causes my words to come out unintelligible, but I'm sure Brazen can decipher the meaning based on how lovingly I bob up and down.

It took years for Brazen to bring me out of a sexual shyness and turn me into his bedroom freak. Now I'm certifiable.

I look up into Brazen's pretty browns while I swallow as much of him as I can without choking on it. I suck him until his pleasure shoots out and coats the back of my throat. I swallow then lick my lips and smile up at him.

"Dayum, Ni! You look freaky as hell with those half glasses on. Lay back and let me take that ass to another galaxy."

Brazen's confidence borders on arrogance but I love it, and he's not frontin'. My boo absolutely knows how to take me there. What Brazen can do with his tongue should be illegal. Just the promise makes my pussy jump.

I lay back, spread my thighs and crook a finger at him.

I softly hum Prince's *Do Me Baby* as Brazen's mouth encircles my nipple and his finger travels the length of my sopping wet pussy. "Oowee!" It feels so dang good.

My honey pot is on fiyah.

The way Brazen sucks my nipples and slides a finger in and out of me has my whole body quivering. His mouth travels down my body and stops right above his fingers. The fluttering of his tongue across my pulsating clit makes me scream out for the Almighty.

"Do you love what I do to your pussy?" he whispers.

The baritone in his voice is an aphrodisiac.

"Dwdagjajptmadj," I cry out.

"Say what?"

"I—don't—know—what I'm saying—Brazen." I breathlessly reply after my volcano erupts with its sweet lava.

Brazen uses his tongue to take me there a second time then he gives me what I'm so addicted to.

Ca$h

CHAPTER 9
Brazen

Ni ain't the only one with an addiction. As much as shorty is addicted to me, I'm just as addicted to hustlin'. That don't mean that paper chasing comes before my girl, it just mean that I can't give up the streets *or* Ni.

A week has passed since me and shorty made up and got back together. I'm in the kitchen whippin' these two bricks I got from Juvie then I'ma drop some weight to a couple of young niggas that I fuck with.

It's Saturday, and Ni is gone somewhere with her cousin, Carmen. Carmen is a short redbone with greenish eyes and a bangin' ass body. She also has a slick ass mouth. Too damn breezy for my taste, but she's Ni's family so I tolerate her.

Anyway, a nigga 'bout to get out here and get that check up. I've been home for two months now so the handouts from muthafuckas have ceased. Now it's time to get it how I live. Ni keeps tryna encourage me to accept a landscaping job with her uncle, but that ain't happening. I'm twenty-six years old and I refuse to mow my *own* lawn so why would I mow the next nigga's? Shorty might as well face it, I'm a hustla for life.

Just as I'm stirring more baking soda into the pot with cocaine, I hear Ni and Carmen coming into the house, engaged in conversation. Before I can hide what I'm doing, they're both in the doorway of the kitchen. They stand on the other side of the L-shaped island grilling me like they've caught me stealing something.

Carmen opens her slick ass mouth first. "Brazen, tell me you're not cooking up drugs in my cousin's house!"

I look at the bitch like I might smash her face in. "I'ma just tell you to find you some business and stay outta mine. Otherwise you can let that door hit you in that high ass of yours," I retort.

"What—eva!" Carmen turns up her lip like a nigga stinks or something. With a flip of her wrist she dismisses my remark about her high sitting ass. "The boys like it," she proclaims.

"Yeah, that's because niggas love easy ass but we don't respect it."

"Who are you calling easy ass? Don't make me pull your card," she says with a roll of her neck.

"Bitch, you don't know nothing about me except you wish you had a nigga like me. Shut the fuck up before we need *First 48* up in this bitch."

I raise my shirt up to expose the burner in my waistband. Carmen's eyes bulge out and she loses all that slick talk.

Ni jumps to her defense, spewing "Brazen that is not cute!"

"Fuck that hoe," I spit.

Carmen storms out of the house.

Now Ni is ranting. Her hands are flying all about and her top lip is curled up. "I cannot believe your ass! Why did you just threaten my cousin with a gun? Have you lost your mind, Brazen? That was so foul. And why do you have drugs in my fuckin' house?" she screams.

"Don't worry, I got this," I assure her. I commence to whipping the work, turning cocaine into crack.

Ca$h

"Brazen, this is just too much! You are going to have to decide whether you want me or that." Ni points to the drugs I have on the counter.

"What you saying?"

"I refuse to allow you to put my life and freedom in jeopardy."

The exasperation in her voice is thicker than old school government cheese. But see, Ni didn't grow up eating that shit. She grew up in a home, I grew up a ward of the state. So all I know is to live off the fat of the land. Ni doesn't seem to understand that, and I'm already tired of her stressin' me to change.

I look shorty in the eye and say, "Nah, baby girl, I don't have to choose. I'ma do what I do. So *you* choose."

When she hesitates to answer I continue on. "I was doing this shit when you met me. Ain't nothing changed but the weight in the pot. So you can either love it or leave it."

My challenge brings water to Ni's eyes. Then she utters her reply…

41

CHAPTER 10
<u>Niesha</u>

Ain' t this a mutha effer! It sets my hair on fire that Brazen is dead ass wrong yet tries to flip shit and put me on the defensive. Well, this is one time I'm standing my ground.

True, I knew that he was a street nigga when we first met him and fell in love back in our sophomore year in high school. But that was ten fuckin' years ago. Come on now! Isn't it time for Brazen to let go of the drug dealing and at least make an attempt at honest work? He can't seem to see there's no future beyond a cemetery or a prison cell in that life.

"Brazen," I say in a calm tone. "Baby, don't you see that when you keep doing the same thing you're going to keep getting the same results? Every time you take one step forward something knocks you three steps back. You go back and forth to prison like you're on some type of doomed merry go round. And I'm tired of

42

it. You promised me that this time would be different. Now look..."

I gesture at the drugs on the kitchen counter and shake my head in exasperation.

All Brazen says is, "This is how I get down, Ni. What, I'm not good enough for you now?" Giving me a hard look as if I've insulted him.

"That's not what I'm saying, Brazen, and you know it!" I yell in frustration.

"Don't try to get brand new on me, shorty. You from the hood, you may have grown up in a house but you could look out your front door and see the projects. You know a hood nigga gotta eat off of the streets."

"That's not true." I refute him.

"Oh, you telling me that muthafuckas with college degrees out there jobless, and you think it's easy for me, a three-time felon, to get a job?"

"My uncle offered to hire you."

"Man, please! I'm not mowing nan muthafuckas lawn. And I'm not tap dancing for no punk ass minimum wage job. I'ma keep fucking with the streets 'til I get rich or die tryin'. Now if you want a 9 to 5 nigga, I might as well step. 'Cause I'm married to the

43

game until it rewards me or kills me," he proclaims selfishly.

"You're disgusting," I say with a scowl.

"Am I? Nawl, I'm real. What you need is some bitch made nigga that'll let you mold him. But you can't mold me," Brazen spits, and pounds his fist against his chest in a show of misunderstood manhood.

My heart falls to the floor because I love Brazen so much but I know what I have to do. Fresh tears burn my eyes and I have to take a deep breath to keep from feeling faint. I realize that I'm going to have to suffer now or suffer later. Might as well let the hurt begin.

"Brazen, I can no longer live like this. You love the streets so go to them. I'm done!" I say pointing towards the door.

Brazen stares at me with a coldness that's chilling. Already I feel bad because he's been abandoned from birth. His mother, whom he has never met, left him at the hospital at two days old. He has no family. No one but the cold streets. Despite it all, I have to let him go.

"This time when I walk out that door I'm not coming back," he threatens and I almost faint.

Can I really live without him? I wonder.

Ca$h

I'm not sure that I can but I'm certain that I would rather try living without Brazen than to wind up his co-defendant or in a coffin alongside of him in a morgue.

So I say to him—this man that I love with all that is me. "Please leave my door key on your way out."

And I am resolute in my tone of delivery.

CHAPTER 11
BRAZEN

Did wifey just tell me to leave the door key on the way out?

Yep, that's what the fuck just came out of her mouth. A'ight, she must think a nigga can't live without her ass. I love shorty but I'm not gonna change in order to please her. She has the game fucked up— I'm the man. I wear the pants.

Until Ni gets back in check and stop listening to her meddling ass relatives I'ma just do me and let her do her. Yep, that's what the fuck I'ma do.

"You gon' regret this baby girl. Trust!" I hurl over my shoulder as I gather up the work that's on the counter then go upstairs to pack my shit for the last and final time.

Shorty ain't finna be puttin' me out every other week. *I'ma get my own spot where can't a muthafucka in the world tell me to get out.* I fume while packing all of my gear into two large carry bags. I leave behind

46

every outfit that Ni bought me. I don't need shit from her.

When I get back downstairs and begin pulling my sneakers and boots out of the hallway closet, I overhear Ni in the living room talking on the phone.

"Yeah Mama, he's packing his things now. I should have heeded your advice years ago when you tried to tell me to let him go and find myself someone who isn't in the streets. Yes ma'am, you're right, he doesn't deserve a good woman like me. I've lied, cried and almost died for him and he still does not appreciate my love. Because if he did, he would at least try to do something honest."

She's looking at me disgusted but I just ignore that shit.

"How can a man claim to love a woman when all he does is cause her heartache? Why should I have to worry about the police or some jack boys kicking my door in, in the middle of the night looking for him? That's no way to live. I just thank God I wasn't dumb enough to have a child with Brazen. Hmmp! He couldn't help me raise a child; he hasn't finished growing up himself."

47

Shorty Got a Thug

As I listen to Ni talk about me like I'm nothing, my eyes turn red. I walk into the living room and find Ni sitting on the couch. I toss the door key in her lap.

"There you go shorty, I'm out!" My voice is venomous.

"Mama let me call you back after I let Brazen out," Ni says into the phone. She ends the call and our eyes meet. Both of our eyes are misty.

I bite my bottom lip tryna control the venom that threatens to come out. I successfully swallow my comment then I slowly head to the door with my bags swung over my shoulder. It takes several trips to carry everything out to my truck. The last thing I carry out is the plastic grocery bag in which I've placed the two bricks.

Now that I don't have to return for anything else, Ni stops me on my way out. "Oh, after ten years of being together you can just leave without giving me a hug and a goodbye kiss." Her voice cracks with emotion that is hard for her to disguise.

I half chuckle, half snarl, "This ain't no movie on Lifetime. Fuck all that dramatic shit. I'm out baby girl. Remember me as you see me now—walking away."

I spin on my heels and stride towards the door. When my hand grips the door knob I feel Ni grab ahold of the back of my shirt.

"Baby, please don't leave. I didn't mean any of what I said. I love you, Brazen. Don't you know that by now?" she cries.

I slap her hands off of me.

Ni slides down to her knees and grips onto my pants leg, begging and crying her eyes out. "I'm sorry Brazen."

I snatch away from her and bounce, leaving her balled up on the floor in a pool of tears.

Fuck Ni! I'm about to hit these streets and get my weight up.

CHAPTER 12

NIESHA

Yeah, I know—I am pitiful, right? I let Brazen pull my strings, rattle my cage, and have me begging him not to leave me when every fiber in my soul tells me I'm better off without him. However, common sense has nothing to do with being in love. I'm so in love with Brazen that I get physically sick when we break up.

In almost every room of the house pictures of us in happier times adorn the wall. Reminders of how wonderful things are when they're at their best. Every love song that plays on my radio reminds me of my boo.

Okay, I'm stupid and I know it.

I look in the mirror and see a beautiful chocolate sistah with a nice shape. I don't have riches but I do have a profession. And I know that I possess a good heart. I can get another man at the blink of an eye, but who wants another man when their heart belongs to the one that's gone?

Ca$h

I think about Brazen every minute of every day. What hurts more than anything is that he can just go on with his life as if I were never a part of it.

"Your ass is just dick whipped, that's all it is," says Carmen. We are seated at the table in my kitchen.

Carmen brought over Chinese carry-out because she knows that I'm depressed and haven't been eating. She has been trying for the past month to hook me up with one guy or another to help me get over Brazen, but my response is always the same—not interested.

"Dick whipped and cum dumb!" Carmen says shaking her head.

"No, it's deeper than sex," I disagree.

Carmen doesn't understand love because she can sex them and keep it moving. And if a nigga ain't caking her she has no further use for him.

"Gurllll, that nigga's dick got you acting like it's made out of platinum or something. But *news flash,* you can get some dick when you can't get anything to eat," Carmen adds.

I try to explain that although Brazen's sex is mind blowing, it's what's inside of him that I love so much.

Shorty Got a Thug

"Ha! What's inside of him? Nothing but a Thug," laughs Carmen. "And that's probably what has you stuck on stupid about him. You made it out of the hood but you can't let go of your hood nigga."

"Carmen, I won't even try to lie—yes, I'm hooked on Brazen's swag, if that's what you mean. But not his profession. I love the side of him that he tries to hide from the world. The tender side of a thug which only true love can bring out. In spite of our battles, no man's love can compare to Brazen's," I say in defense of him.

Carmen's hand shoots to her forehead in mock exasperation. "How would you know? Brazen's dick is the only one you've ever had," she scoffs.

"It's not about dick, it's about love Carmen. But I'm going to force myself to let go because this is not the way love should feel. Anyway, after the things I said, I'm sure that I've lost Brazen forever."

"Lost him! Lost him!" explodes Carmen. "Chick, do you hear yourself? How could you lose Brazen? That nigga has never belonged to you, he belongs to the streets. That's where he was when you met him and that is where he'll die."

"Don't say that!"

"Why not? You know it's the truth," she shouts, hands on her hips.

"It is not. And stop saying that."

My voice raises to a feverish pitch and we shout back and forth, calling each other names, and slinging food across the table at one another.

After a long moment of silence during which our tempers cool down, Carmen apologizes. "I'm sorry boo, I just don't want to see you hurt. You know I love you, we're family."

"You're right, and you're also right about Brazen, but now is not the time, okay?"

"I understand. Now bend down and let me get that rice out of your hair."

"Um—you have some in your hair too." I say and we both laugh.

We hug and the disagreement is forgotten.

A week later I'm on the phone with Carmen. We're discussing a guy named Tori who Carmen hooked me up with. Tori is thirty years old. He's tall, handsome, single with no children, and he's into commercial development. We've gone out once to a jazz bar and from there, dinner at Justin's. It was an enjoyable evening but Brazen was on my mind the entire time.

"I'm supposed to go over to Tori's house out in Clarkston and watch a movie with him, but I don't know if I'm going to go," I say, hedging.

"Girl, you're just scared he's gonna ask for some pussy," jokes Carmen.

"I am not. But if he does try to take it there, I'll have to shut him down. I am not ready for anything like that."

"If I were you I'd give Tori some. Some half decent dick might help relieve your stress. Best believe Brazen has not kept his dirty dick on the shelf. He's probably running up in every trick that opens her legs for him. So ain't no sense in you walking around with a lonely pussy, thinking you'd be doing him wrong if you get a little bit. Until you cum for another man you'll never get over Brazen."

Carmen swears that she's a freakin' love doctor. Sometimes I want to cover my ears and scream at her advice.

So why is it, later that night, I'm on Tori's bed with my panties down?

Ca$h

I squeeze my eyes shut as Tori goes down on me. I feel like the biggest ho' in Atlanta!

I push his head from between my thighs and pull my panties back up. "I'm sorry but I can't do this," I apologize sincerely, hoping he'll understand.

At first he tries to sweet talk me into letting him continue. When I refuse, it quickly turns ugly.

Tori grabs me by the hair and growls, "Oh, because my pants don't sag off my ass and I don't pack a glock, I don't turn you on?"

"Oh no, please don't take it like that. I'm sorry but I never should have come here tonight. Now will you please turn my hair aloose?" I plead.

Instead of letting my hair go Tori yanks it tighter.

"Oww! You're hurting me!" I scream at him.

"Oh, you ain't felt nothing yet!" he replies.

Oh God, how did I get myself into this situation?

If only Brazen hadn't left me.

CHAPTER 13

Niesha

Somehow I manage to snatch myself free of Tori's grip. My scalp is stinging where a few strands of my hair was yanked out in the process. I stand up and shove Tori away from me, and the next thing I know I'm on the floor and the room is spinning.

A bloody mouth and the stinging sensation across my cheek confirms that this negro just slapped the shit out of me.

He snarls, "Since you obviously like niggas who dog your ass out, I'ma do just that!"

He grabs me by the collar of my blouse and barks, "Get naked, ho!"

The room is spinning faster now as I try to get to my feet and fight him off. The fuck if this weak bastard is going to get away with putting his ball scratchers on me!

I pounce on him like an alley cat. I'm clawing at his face and trying to knee him in the balls. "Ahhhh!" Tori yelps when my long nails dig into his eyes. "Bitch, you're going to blind me!"

56

"You're mutha effin right I'ma blind your ass! Then I'm going to make sure your mother has to bury you," I spit.

I'm in a rage. I try to detach his retinas.

Suddenly a fist slams into my face and I go down like a sack of bricks. Tori chokes me until I momentarily pass out. When I regain consciousness my panties are off and I'm being forcefully violated.

"You dope-boy-lovin' bitch. You don't want to give a real man no pussy so I'm taking it. I'm going to dog your hoe ass out like that nigga did," grunts Tori as he pushes in and out of me savagely.

I scream but no one can hear me because the music is just as loud as my scream. When did he turn the music on? I wonder as bile rises up in my throat.

I throw up all over Tori.

Suddenly he stops raping me. He gets up off of me and sits on the edge of the bed with his head in his hands. "Niesha, I am so sorry. I have never forced myself on a woman before, and I have never laid hands on a woman."

I run off to the bathroom and throw up all over the toilet. I'm crying so hard that my chest heaves in and out. It takes me a long while to regain my composure. When I do, I return to the bedroom where this raping bastard is still sitting on the edge of the bed sobbing into his hands.

Shorty Got a Thug

I walk up close to him and raise the straight razor
that I found in the bathroom.

"You bastard!" I cry as I slash him across the face.

CHAPTER 14

<u>Brazen</u>

"Yo, stop with the games. If Ni is tryna get me to come back home she should be able to come up with a more believable story than that. Carmen, y'all are too funny!" I laugh dismissively at what Ni's cousin just told me.

"I'm not kidding, Brazen," she insist.

"Yeah—yeah—yeah! And I'm working at the White House! Girl stop with the bullshit, why would shorty be in jail?" I chuckle at the lunacy of what Carmen is telling me.

Carmen and Ni must think I'm slow. They better tighten up their game. I know this is just Ni's desperate plea for my attention but after all of that woo-woo shit Ni said about me to her mother, I'm straight done with baby girl.

"No, Brazen, I'm as serious as a fuckin' heart attack. This is not a prank. I wouldn't be calling your phone playing games. Remember, I don't even like you! Niesha needs someone to bail her out of jail and I don't have all of the money. She doesn't want her mother to know about this so you're her only option," explains Carmen.

I turn the music down in my truck so that I can hear clearly what Carmen is saying. I'm headed out to Gresham Road to handle some business but that can be put on hold if Ni is in some type of trouble.

"What is she locked up for?" I question Carmen.

"I'll let Niesha tell you herself."

Now my mind is wondering all kinds of craziness. Though I don't fuck with Ni anymore I'm not gonna turn my back on her. Every time I ever got locked up shorty came through for me.

Suspense is killing me. I press Carmen for details. She finally divulges that Ni is charged with aggravated assault and attempted murder.

"What?" I can't believe my ears.

"That's all I can tell you. You'll have to ask Niesha for the details when we bail her out if you want to know more," says Carmen.

"Yo, why the fuck you being so secretive?" I spazz on her but it does no good because Carmen simply ignores the question. "Anyway, how much is her bond?" I ask.

"A hundred thousand."

"Whew!"

Ca$h

"But we can take the bondsman ten percent and they'll bond her out. I have twenty-five hundred. Do you have seventy-five hundred?"

I'm insulted.

"That ain't a problem," I respond. I don't hustle for the hell of it. Of course I got seven and a half racks. "In fact you can hold on to your money, I got this," I add.

"Fine. When will you be able to get with me?"

"Right away. Let me hit my dude up and put this move on hold. I'll be by your crib to pick you up in twenty minutes."

On the way to scoop Carmen up so we can go to the bondsman's office, I can't help wondering who in the hell did Ni attempt to murder, and why? I hit my man up and tell him I'll have to get at him later because something important has come up. Then I dash over to Carmen's so that we can go rescue my little damsel in distress.

We wait at the bondsman's office for hours only to be told that we won't be able to bond Ni out until 7 A.M.

61

Shorty Got a Thug

My Rolex reads 2:00 A.M. on the dot.

By the time we reach Carmen's house it's 2:55A.M.

"If you wanna crash on my sofa so you won't have to drive all the way back in a couple of hours, you're welcome to. Under the circumstances," Carmen offers.

Now that's real generous coming from a bitch that can't stand me. Since I'm already tired I accept the offer.

Damn! Is that a smile I see on Carmen's face?

CHAPTER 15

Carmen

I fluff up a bed pillow and lay it on the couch along with a clean bed sheet.

"Will you be comfortable? I know the couch is small and you have long legs so if it feels too cramped I guess you can sleep at the foot of my bed," I offer Brazen as I watch him remove his shirt.

He doesn't respond.

"Did you hear me?" I ask, standing in front of him with nothing on but a big tee that functions as a comfortable nightie. My legs are slightly agape.

Brazen says, "I'm good." Like he can't see all of this woman standing before him.

Honestly, I have always been attracted to this nigga, I just hid it real well. I wanna know if his dick is really as good as my cousin claims. I'm hoping that at the very least he'll make me come.

My pussy is jumping and I'm sure he can smell my feminine desire. Can it be that he has no attraction to me? *Hell to the na, it can't be that.* I'm a sexy red bitch, much prettier than black ass Niesha.

I try to keep the disappointment off of my face as I accept the rejection and turn and go to my bedroom. I throw my hips like a stripper ascending a staircase, making my ass cheeks bounce with each step I take.

In my bedroom I put on a pair of six inch stilettos and strip down to nothing else. I'm determined to seduce Brazen, whatever it takes. A bad bitch like myself can seduce an impotent saint so there's no way a street nigga can turn all of *this* down. I do not do rejection well. In fact, I have very little experience in that regard. I promise, I'm about to get fucked.

I saunter back into the living room displaying all of my 38 Ds, small waist and 42 inch hips. My bald pussy mound is fat and throbbing between my thighs. Brazen is stretched out on the couch, eyes closed. I sit down on the edge of the couch, press a bare thigh against his leg, and run my hands all over his toned chest.

"Yo—what the fuck!" he exclaims, bolting up.

I grab his hand and look into his eyes. "I couldn't sleep," I stammer.

Ca$h

"Carmen, you need to put some muthafuckin' clothes on. Fa real, li'l mama, why you tryin' a nigga?" Brazen hotly protests.

"C'mon baby boy, don't act surprised. I'm sure you know I've been frontin' all this time—a bitch been craving some of this for years."

I slide my hands inside his unbuttoned jeans and wrap my hand around his grown man. Dayum! So this is why Niesha is so gone over him. I'm stroking Brazen's dick as I lean down and brush my excited nipples across his mouth.

"We can fuck each other's brains out, Brazen, and my cousin doesn't ever have to find out. I just wanna feel all of this dick deep inside this fat pussy."

"Shorty, you on that bullshit!" he says.

He attempts to push me up off of him, but not very convincingly.

"Brazen, let me suck this big dick." My voice is husky with desire as I stroke that mutha slow and firm.

"Nah, this shit ain't gucci," Brazen begins but now I have the head in my mouth and what nigga can resist that? I spit right on the head of that dick and his resistance evaporates.

65

Shorty Got a Thug

I pull his jeans and boxers down so that I can really get to it, balls included. When I feel his hands gripping my head I know the battle has been won. In no time at all I'm swallowing tiny little Brazens. "Did you enjoy that?" I ask him as I stroke him back to rock hardness.

He doesn't answer me. He doesn't have to. The answer just splashed down my throat.

I stand up and show him all pussy, spreading my delicate lips, and caressing my clit until she peeks out of her hood.

"Isn't my coochie pretty? You wanna put your dick up inside of me and fuck me like I'm a ho? C'mon, baby, this pussy is dying for you."

Brazen pulls me down on top of him then flips me over onto my back. He enters me roughly but it feels so damn good to a bitch as he goes deep, deep, deep, deep.

Brazen goes deeper than any other nigga has gone before, and our rhythms match perfectly and animalistically at the same time. This dick feels like the Proclamation of Emancipation—it's going to free me!

I cry out, "Ooh, Brazen, your dick is my salvation!"

He grumbles and pounds harder.

Ca$h

"Ooh—shit! You hear my pussy calling out your name? Does Ni's pussy get this wet and grip this tight?" I challenge.

"Her shit is way tighter," he replies coldly.

If he wasn't making me feel so good I would cuss his ass out.

"Take it out and put it in my ass. Let's see if you like how tight *that* is," I offer.

Brazen tries to run up in my ass but he's too big. I direct him to some lubricant that's inside the adjoining bathroom. He comes back greased up, then he applies some all over my crinkle. He enters me slowly. Once he is comfortably inside, it feels so good, I see stars and bubbles.

"Yessss, baby, fuck this tight ass," I half cry, half plead.

"You know this some foul shit we doin' to Ni." His words speak of his regret but he sure hasn't stopped dicking me down.

"Uh—huh—but—who—cares? It—feels—good," I moan and throw this ass back at that dick. I want to make him nut so hard that he'll call my name in his goddamn sleep.

Shorty Got a Thug
I am determined to make Brazen mine.

CHAPTER 16

<u>Niesha</u>

I'm sitting in a stinky jail cell with four other women, all of whom look like they could use a shower and some bug spray. I've cried so much that my eyes are swollen and my voice is hoarse.

After slicing Tori up, from ass crack to throat, I called 911. When the police arrived with EMTs and questioned me about what happened, I replied with no remorse, "I gutted that mutha effer!"

"Why?" asked the cop, looking down at the bloody mess that the emergency technicians were hurrying into the back of the ambulance.

"Because he tried to take what he had no right to," I replied, showing no remorse.

So here I sit in jail waiting for Carmen to post my bail.

A negro rapes me and *I* get arrested! I cannot believe I'm in jail!

What's taking Carmen so long?

Shorty Got a Thug

A butch chick sits next to me on the cold steel bench and her funk greets me before she does.

"Hi cutie. You need a friend?" she ask. She resembles Cuba Gooding.

"No, I just want to be left alone." I drop my head back down. I don't want to look her in the eye because she could mistake it for interest.

"Did you and your boyfriend have a fight?"

"No! I just tried to kill someone for forcing himself on me—take heed!"

Butch chick does exactly that.

Trust, I am not the bitch to be trifled with right now!

I spring to my feet when a deputy calls my name and tells me that my bond has been posted. When I walk through the last door that separates me from freedom, and enter the lobby, I'm shocked to find Brazen there with Carmen. *Oh my God! Has she told him what happened? Everything?*

How on earth did these two get along long enough to bail me out? I wonder. Carmen hates Brazen and he feels the same way about her. I guess they have put their differences aside for the time being.

Ca$h

As soon as Carmen hugs me I burst out in tears. "Thank you for everything," I cry, hugging her tightly.

"It's okay chick," she cajoles me. Then she looks at Brazen and smiles with a friendliness that's astonishing to me.

I turn and say to Brazen in a tone that comes out like phlegm, "Thank you too." Then I look down at the floor in shame, wondering if Carmen has told him that I was raped.

On the way out to his truck Brazen ask, "What happened?"

My response gets stuck in my throat when Carmen sits up front with *my* man.

I slam the back door and hiss, "I don't feel up to discussing it!"

Silence fills the truck. Not another word is spoken by anyone until Brazen drops me and Carmen off at her house. Getting out of his truck, I see hickies on his neck. "You are so disrespectful!" I cry as I slam the door.

Carmen stays in the truck with Brazen another five minutes before joining me on her doorsteps. When she goes to unlock the front door, her shoulder length hair falls to the side and I notice hickies on her neck too.

"Oh hell no! I'm going back to jail!"

Ca$h

CHAPTER 17
<u>Carmen</u>

Soon as me and Niesha get inside my apartment she whirls around and steps all up in my face, looking me up and down like a FDA inspector. She moves my hair back and closely examines my neck.

My heart beats fast because I know what she's looking at. There's faint hickies on my neck. Hours ago, after Brazen pulled out of my gooey ass, I straddled that dick and made this pussy drop, pop, and roll. We were both so caught up that we tried to devour each other.

Niesha doesn't mince her words; I give cuz her due. "Bitch, did you fuck my man?" she ask straight out.

"Huh?"

"Ho, if you can huh you can hear. Why is it that you and Brazen both have hickies?" she demands to know.

I put my hands on my hips and roll my eyes. "Chick, you got me twisted. I was getting fucked real good last night by a baller I met at the club last week, until you called me with your drama. I don't know what Brazen's story is but

73

best believe his dirty dick hasn't been up in this prime nookie. Anyway, is this the thanks I get for coming to get you out?"

My response works. Niesha swallows my deception whole. "I'm sorry, girl. My mind is thrown all the way off right now," she apologizes. Then she tearfully recounts what happened with Tori and her.

"Is he going to live?" I ask. I pray that he doesn't then little cousin-poo will be out of my way. I need Brazen's dick all to myself.

"I don't know if that bastard is going to live or not, and right now I don't care—forgive me Lord," replies Niesha.

"Well, why were *you* arrested?"

"It was a formality until the detectives can talk to Tori and sort things out," she explains.

A devious idea pops in my mind. *Hmm! That just might work.*

CHAPTER 18

Niesha

After talking with Carmen I go and take a much needed shower and try to clear my mind of all that has happened the past twelve hours.

Standing under the shower in my cousin's guest bathroom, I have a long cry. My tears mix with the shower water that drips down to the drain and disappear into oblivion. But pain and strong suspicion still remains. I swear I could see right through Carmen's phony explanation.

Okay, she wants to be devious! I snort as I dry off and retire to the spare bedroom where I unsuccessfully try to find sleep. I'm haunted by visions of what Tori did to me. I feel so violated. Adding to that is my strong suspicion concerning Carmen and Brazen.

The morning sun peeks through the open blinds. After gathering my thoughts I call Brazen.

"Who dis?" he answers as if he no longer has my phone number listed in his contacts.

I speak my suspicions as if they have already been admitted to and confirmed.

"Brazen, out of all the lowdown trifling things you have done this is the grimiest. I cannot believe you are so fuckin' foul as to sleep with my freakin' cousin. *My cousin, Brazen*!" My voice is low but harsh, and certain of what I'm accusing him of.

Brazen feigns cool under assault.

"Ni, what are you talkin' about? Are you crazy?" he laughs.

Yep, he fucked that trick bitch! I automatically conclude. Because I know Brazen like I know the curves of my own body. If I was accusing him of something that he wasn't guilty of he would snap. He hates to be falsely accused. He hasn't cussed me out and hung up the phone because he needs to hear my proof. That's his freakin' m.o.

"Shorty, you know I—"

"Don't you dare try to lie, nigga! Carmen is right here next to me and she's told me everything!" I go off.

Brazen gets quiet. Finally he replies, "Oh, yeah? Well, did the bitch tell you that she came on to me? I kept trynna tell her that that was some foul shit but she wouldn't fall back, she just had to have my dick in her mouth. Anyway, me and you ain't together so don't worry about who I fuck."

"What? After I've loved your ass for ten years, this is how you do me? *My cousin Brazen?* I hate you!"

I hang up the phone and collapse back down on the bed, crying like never before. This is the worst betrayal imaginable. And I'm being served it from both sides. What did I ever do to deserve this? I bury my face in the pillow and ask the Man above.

There is no divine answer—nothing but the muffled sounds of my broken heart.

When my sobs subside I get up and storm into Carmen's bedroom. I find her asleep as if she has not betrayed me. I pull the cover off of her and she startles awake, blinking those eyes that's centered in her two-faced mug.

I smash her in the mouth with my fist.

"Wake up, you slimy ho and take this ass whooping standing up!" I grab a handful of her hair and yank her to her feet.

"Ahh!" She cries out.

I let go of her hair and release these twins on her ass. I pummel her face with both fist, getting my Laila Ali on.

"For a backstabbing bitch with no morals and a lying tongue, you don't put up much fight," I mock as I three piece her while bouncing up and down on my toes.

Whop! Whop! Whop! Bap! Bap! Bap! My fists connect with her face repeatedly. Carmen tries to swing back but she can't touch this! She's one of those cute bitches that can't fight.

I kick her ass until I'm out of breath. I sit down for a minute, catch my breath. Think about Carmen fucking my man. Hop up and get some more of that jaw.

"I hope the dick was good, bitch! Because I'm still going to be beating this ass when Jesus returns."

I beat Carmen to a pulp.

Then I call Brazen.

"What!" He has the nerve to answer with an attitude.

"If you want Carmen you can come and scrape the bitch up of the floor!"

CHAPTER 19

Carmen

Dayuuummmmm! I forgot that Niesha can fight like a man. That chick woke me up to an ass whoopin' that I'll never forget. But let's see who is victorious in the end.

I'ma see just how tough she is when she goes to prison for trying to kill Tori. Oh, it'll happen if I have my way.

Right now I'm lying across my bed with and ice pack on my left eye. That heifer socked me often and hard. I'm sore from the top of my head down to my feet. I'm hurting places she didn't even hit me. Feeling woozy but still determined to lay a claim to Brazen, I find my cell phone and hit Brazen up.

He answers with a funky attitude.

"What's wrong with you?" I ask.

"Yo, why the fuck you gotta kiss and tell?"

"Hold up nigga! I ain't tell that bitch nothing. I thought you did."

"Say what? Damn! If you didn't say nothing, Ni played me," he quickly deduces.

I tell Brazen how Niesha beat the crap out of me and he roars with laughter.

"It's not funny Brazen. I'm laying here all jacked up. I'm too cute for this shit," I pout.

"You want me to come through there later and make you feel better?" offers Brazen. His concern automatically makes me feel a little better. I imagine him babying me.

"You owe me a whole lot of TLC because you're to blame for me getting my butt kicked. You let Niesha trick you into admitting everything. Who does that?"

Brazen laughs. "Yeah, I slipped. But I'ma make it up to you. Do you promise to make that ass clap like you did earlier?"

I giggle. "Any way you want it, daddy," I coo.

Hours later I answer the door to let Brazen in. He takes one look at my swollen eye and remarks, "Goddamn shorty, don't you know how to duck?"

He cracks up as he gently strokes my cheek.

"It's not funny!" I wrinkle my nose up and walk into his open arms. Niesha might have gotten the best of me but I have her boo.

Ca$h

Tonight I'm going to fuck Brazen with all that I have. This pussy is going to make him forget all about Niesha. Then tomorrow I'm going to the hospital and pay Tori a visit. Together we're going to fix Niesha!

CHAPTER 20

Brazen

It's been a full week since Ni stomped a mud hole in Carmen's ass. The soreness is gone but there's still discoloration under the eye that was blackened. That's because shorty is one of those high yellow broads. But she'll be gucci soon.

I've been showing Carmen mad love, and I keep the dick up in her, but it's not what everyone thinks. Nah, I'm not pussy trapped. Neva that. Trust I got a game plan.

Ni might hate me right now for fuckin' with her people but I never worry about shorty, we're always gonna be good. Our thing is unconditional, I just gotta do me for a minute. Me and Ni will end back up together but now is not the time because the streets are calling and ya boy has to answer.

For the moment Carmen serves a purpose. The same can be said for my partner Juvie. With one exception—Juvie's purpose has been served. I'm in good with Juvie's connect and I have my own clientele and a team on deck. So Juvie is expendable.

Yeah, I know his punk ass tried to get at Ni when I was on lock. Carmen recently told me about it. So Juvie's fate is sealed.

Me and Juvie are at his kitchen table staring at ten bricks and fifty stacks. "Yeah, homie, we about to get this check," Juvie boast, and the light in the kitchen reflects off his grill.

The nigga is smiling but in a minute I'm gonna turn that smile into a frown.

I look at him sinisterly. "Fam, the only thing you 'bout to get is fitted for a coffin."

Juvie's brows furrow, then his face goes ashen when he sees my hand gripping a Glock .50.

"You ain't gotta take nothin' from me, bruh. If I eat, you eat," he pleads.

I stand up still holding the burner on him, and hock a glob of spit in his face. "Save the bullshit, homie. Nigga, you was out here eating hella good while I was on lock barely able to make commissary unless Ni looked out. Shorty made sure I had what I needed but she had to go without shit she needed in order to make it happen."

Shorty Got a Thug

"I ain't know that, bruh," he lies, and his eyes water. But really that nigga ain't got no feelings and his fakeness infuriates me.

"Bitch, you didn't care. Plus, you's a grimey-type nigga. You stepped to my shorty on some real fuckery while I was away. What, you didn't think I would find out that you tried to fuck Ni? Go ahead and deny it so I can scramble ya shit!" Spittle is flying out of my mouth I'm so heated.

From the look on his face I can tell that he's thinking about denying it. But he knows that I don't bark, I bite.

"Bruh, I'm sorry. In spite of all of that, you know I got love for you," he whines.

"Tell it to God!" I spit, then pop two in his thinker. He topples over backwards in the chair. I stand over him and do him real bad. Boc! Boc! Boc!

"Bitch made ass nigga," I snarl looking down at his brains on my shoe.

I calmly snatch up the work and the cheddar, and I'm in the wind.

CHAPTER 21

Niesha

My mouth hits the floor when I see on the news that Juvie has been brutally murdered. My concern is that maybe Brazen's life is in danger since he and Juvie were so close.

Maybe I'm plain dumb for still caring about Brazen but I can't help how I feel. Regardless to how trifling Brazen's betrayal with my cousin is, I wish him no harm. Things have not always been this bad between us. Yes, he's been back and forth to prison throughout the entire ten years we were together but there has been plenty of good times. There was a time when Brazen put my wants over everything.

All I have to do is close my eyes and the happy memories play in my mind with such visual clarity, I can't help but show my teeth. My very first everything includes that man. So I can't just erase him from my heart like some unwanted text message that shows up on the screen of my cell phone. I love him with my heart and soul. However, I love myself too. Therefore, I refuse to play the fool for him.

I do want him to know that I am concerned about him, which is why I'm parked outside of the church where Juvie's wake is being held. Somber mourners trickle out one behind the other as the service comes to an end. I spot Brazen walking out with Juvie's mother. He gives her a hug then walks towards his truck with his head down and both hands shoved in his pockets.

Brazen spots me. He opens the passenger door to my Altima and slides inside. In spite of all that's going on he looks good, and I don't hesitate to tell him so.

"You're looking good too, baby" he rasps.

Instantly I began longing for him. I fight off my reverie because in my mind's eye I keep seeing him making love to Carmen.

"I'm sorry about Juvie," I offer my condolences. "I won't pretend that I liked him but still I feel sorry for his family."

"All maggots get crushed eventually."

Brazen's response startles me. I'm too lost to come back with a rejoiner.

We sit in the car and talk long after all the other cars have gone. Brazen tells me, "Ni, I know I'm dead ass wrong for fucking wit' Carmen, and if the shoe was on the other foot, I'd be calling you all types of hoes and rats. I'm not gonna try to justify what can't be justified. Straight up, a nigga let his dick rule his mind."

Tears trickle down my face. I turn my head to hide my pain.

"Are you seeing her now?" I ask him.

"Yeah, I ain't gon' lie. But I got something for that scut bucket ho. I'ma use her for a purpose that you're way too good for. Then I'ma fix things with you and me," I tries to explain.

I look into Brazen's eyes and see sincerity. But he's lost his damn mind if he thinks I'm supposed to be okay with that. With a curled lip I say, "No Brazen, there is no way to repair this type of betrayal and disrespect."

"Please don't talk like that, baby girl," he pleads. Then he gently takes my face in his hands and stares into my tear-filled eyes. "I'm gonna fix it Ni. I don't know how or when, but I will. I just need to get this check proper so I can give you everything you deserve, then I'm walking away from these streets and all the other shit that makes me break your heart. In the meantime I'm using any and everybody else. Don't give up on me baby. Please. I love you so much."

Shorty Got a Thug

He kisses me before I can object.

As he pulls back I see a tear trickle down his face. Then he's out of the car in a flash.

Is he being sincere or running game? How can he ask me to understand him fucking my cousin?

"Brazen!" I yell after him. "Goodbye forever."

My words mean nothing at all to him. He stops and yells over his shoulder, "I'll be back for you, Ni."

CHAPTER 22
CARMEN

Several weeks ago Tori was released from the hospital only to be arrested and charged with rape. As soon as I heard the news, I made a beeline to the Gwinnett County jail where he was being held in lieu of a $50,000 bond.

I told him that I was willing to concoct a story about Niesha confessing to me that she and Tori had consensual sex and afterwards she snapped because of a text Tori received from another woman.

"But that's not true," he whispered.

It's a good thing there was a glass partition between us or I would've busted his nose.

"Tori, do you want to go to prison and end up being some nigga's bitch?" I'd hissed.

"No, but I forced—"

"Shut up!" I cut him off. Looking around to see if anybody was listening. "Look at you! Your face looks like fucking pinstripes!"

89

"I deserved it." He begins bawling.

"Shut your stupid mouth! Now let me tell you what happened."

By the time the visit was over, I had convinced Tori to go along with my devious scheme.

My next plan was to tell Brazen the same story to turn him against Niesha. When I do, Brazen discounts it totally.

He says, "Nah, Ni wouldn't give up the pussy. And she damn sho' wouldn't have snapped like that over no other bitch. Shorty ain't that shot out over nan nigga but me."

Silently, I'm seething. I toss more salt on it.

"Whatever the truth is, I do know that they did have sex and it wasn't the first time."

Brazen's face turns to stone.

"Ni told you that?"

I nod yes. Still, he discounts it.

"I don't believe that. Shorty would never do that until she was one hundred percent certain that it was over between us. I know my shorty."

I'm so mad my teeth rattle.

"Who is your shorty?" I challenge his black ass by giving him a she-devil look, complete with the upturned lip and claws ready to lash out.

"Be easy, boo. You know what I meant. It's all about *you* right now."

"Nigga it better be," I frown.

"Check this out: I need to know if you gon' ride for a nigga, cause I'm about to go hard after this check, and I need a thorough bitch on my team. If you ain't gonna ride hard, I can't fuck with you. That's why I had to bounce Ni. She wasn't willing to hold me down in this street shit no more," claims Brazen.

"Boo, you never have to worry about that with me. I'ma have your back no matter what," I swear.

"We'll see," he says.

He begins to undress me. His touch sends a bolt of fire straight between my thighs. While Brazen lays me back on my bed and circles my nipple with his tongue, I'm wondering what all he expects of me when he says I'll need to be his rider.

Later, after I've been fucked silly, Brazen tells me the first thing that he needs me to do for him. With a wet ass and a stretched pussy, my silly ass agrees to do it.

CHAPTER 23
<u>Brazen</u>

It straight up makes a nigga feel bad to have to take Ni through all the drama I'm putting her through. I know shorty loves the ground I walk on and the feeling is mutual.

Six years ago, her pops was dying from prostate cancer, he made me promise to take care of his only child and to give her the world. I looked in that dying man's eyes and made that promise and I'ma keep it. Ni's father wasn't a street dude, but he never tried to judge me for the way I got mine. He knew, despite the fuckery, I loved his daughter like no other.

Sometimes it feels like ol' boy is looking down, wagging his finger at me. I just look up to the heavens, smile, and say, "Don't worry old man, there's a method to my madness."

Many people might not understand how I'm rockin' but the end will justify the means.

Carmen?

Ca$h

That bitch ain't nothin' but a pawn. We just got finished enjoying a cozy dinner at this Mexican restaurant off of Buford Highway. We bounce from there, walking to the car, hand in hand, then we catch a movie.

Now it's around midnight and we're rollin' to the Westside in the hood where I grew up. It's dark out and ain't nothing moving but fiends and criminals. As I drive down Simpson Road and turn on Ashby Road, I suddenly say to Carmen, "Tomorrow I'ma need you to make that move for me."

Carmen knows what move I'm referring to, since we just discussed it over dinner.

I'll be sending her to Miami with a hundred stacks to cop some work from my connect. I can't make the trip myself, because I'm already a three-time loser, another drug charge would get me life in the pen. I can't chance riding I-85—cocaine lane—dirty like that. Highway patrol be all over young black men.

I look over in the passenger seat and say to Carmen, "I know you say that I can trust you, but a hunnid stacks can temp *God.* I'ma need for you to understand that there's two things I don't play about—my money and my cheddar."

"Aren't those one and the same?" asks Carmen.

Shorty Got a Thug

"So, you get my point?"

"Yes, Brazen."

I nod my head and say, "I hear you. Now I'm about to *show* you what I mean."

I pull up to the curb behind a clucker who's lookin' down at the ground like he's lost something.

"Say homes! You wanna make a fiddy spot?" I yell out the window.

The clucker looks up and answers. "How?"

"Go cop me some hard." I wave a fist full of money out of the window.

Sensing an easy mark, the crack head nigga walks up to the driver's door of my truck. As soon as he leans down to look inside the truck I press my Glock against his forehead and spray his brains up in the air. His body drops to the pavement, twisted.

I ain't done.

I hop out of the truck—*Boc! Boc!* The clap of the Glock is loud in the quiet of the midnight hour.

When I hop back in the truck and peel off, Carmen's loud screams assault my ears. "Shut up!" The Glock is aimed at her face.

She covers her mouth with both hands and hides her head in her lap. Crying and trembling.

Ca$h

I force her head up so that our eyes meet, and in a calm, even tone I say, "I smashed that nigga for no reason. Imagine what you'll get if you play wit' my duckets."

Her face is almost white

CHAPTER 24
CARMEN

Lord Jesus!

What have I gotten myself into? I'm wondering as Brazen takes the gun away from my head. This diabolical thug has just killed a man simply to make his point clear to me. Oh Jesus Lord God Almighty!

Brazen pops in a Plies CD and cruises to the beat with a calm that is frightening . . . if I was your average bitch. But since I'm not, I lift my head out of my lap and regain my composure.

"Look in the ashtray and spark that blunt for me," says Brazen.

I'm so turned on by his gangsta my thong is wet. I spark the blunt and pass it to him. He takes a few tokes then tosses it out of the window.

"You good, li'l mama?" he inquires.

"I'm good," I assure him. "Baby, I would never take from you."

"It wouldn't be wise."

Ca$h

My response is to put my face in his lap and show him how turned on I am by the killa shit in him. I dome him up real good, until I'm swallowing the rewards.

"Umm, baby, your seeds taste like apricot." I smack my lips savoring the taste of his nut.

"You just a freak," he chuckles.

"You complaining?" I tease.

"Nah, I like keepin' this dick down your throat. You can't talk breezy with a mouthful of wood."

"Brazen, you say the nicest things." My facetiousness makes him smile. He knows that he has me open.

What he doesn't know is that now he's mine! Let him ever try to leave me and go back to that bitch. Watch how fast I go tell that! Brazen will forever belong to me or he'll forever belong to the Bureau of Prisons.

I smile back at him sweetly and purr, "I wonder if you realize that I'm in love with you." *And that you can never leave me.*

Ha! Ha!

CHAPTER 25

<u>BRAZEN</u>

Love? *Bitch just play your position*, I was thinking that night in the truck.

Since then Carmen has made several trips to M-I-yayo for me and now I got them thangs on deck. 'Bout to put the game under foot. Get this check and get out the game. I'm not tryna be in the game for years because I already know how quickly the tide can turn.

There's several teams from Nawlins and some Mexican niggas who have a grip on the A, and they all have phenomenal murder games. That ain't no problem to me, I'm sick with that clap clap myself and I'm going after that ass. Gonna return the A to its rightful owners, native ATLiens.

I've put together a team of boss hustlas and killas that can't be fucked wit', and we're all hungry and ready to eat.

Ca$h

I look around the basement of the house we're at for the purpose of tonight's meeting. In a fold up chair to my right is Silk, a twenty-two year old head banger from The Bluff who resembles a young Snoop Dogg, minus that wack ass perm. Silk ain't no rapper though. The only thing he knows about rapping is wrapping bodies up.

I've known Silk for five years and his get down is official. My only concern with Silk is that he's a born leader, and can't but one captain steer this ship. And that's me.

Since Silk's murder game is so nice I'm letting him roll with the squad despite my misgivings. But at the first sign of treason I'ma do what I gotta do.

To Silk's right is Fat Cat. Nigga big as a house. He not a killa and his swag is dim, but he knows how to flip that work. Then there's Butta and Dee, a lesbian couple from Zone One. They posted up at the li'l bar against the wall. Dee is twenty-five years old and strictly veggie. Shorty think she got a real dick. But that's my peeps because she is *ten toes down,* and she goes hard in the paint. She rocks a short 'fro, and she dresses straight like a dude. Dee will slump a nigga quick if he fucks with her money or her bitch.

Which brings me to Butta.

Butta gonna get a muthafucka eulogized, 'cause li'l mama is a bad ass bitch and mad dudes be tryna holla. She's only 5'2" or so but she's pretty as hell. She is light brown complexioned with exotic eyes and sweet juicy lips. She changes hair styles regularly and always smells scrumptious. And her body is stacked!

Dee spoils Butta tryna keep Butta's mind off of real dick, but Butta knows how to get her duckets too. And don't be fooled by li'l mama's size or looks, baby done napped her share of niggas.

Across from Butta sits Tank, whose name is justified. Homie is built like a tank. He's a real loyal dude who set aside his own grind to get down with the team.

Finally there's Unc, an old head who used to be major out here before serving a fifteen year bid. Unc came home from the feds last year and quickly found out that shit had changed, young niggas regulating the game now. I put him on the team so that we all could sponge his wisdom.

Ca$h

I look over my squad then call the meeting to order and everybody kills the chatter. We're all seated around a square table on which forty bricks are stacked. I'm seated at the head of the table, of course. I'm the Don.

I say, "Everybody already knows one another so ain't no need for introductions. I told y'all a few weeks ago that I was finna put something real big together, and there it is in front of you."

I'm indicating the forty bricks of fish scale.

"That's just the beginning. Before it's all said and done we gonna be running the city," I add confidently.

"Now that's wassup!" chimes in Dee.

"Our team gonna lock shit down!" That's Butta echoing her boo's enthusiasm.

Fat Cat asks, "What are we gonna call our team? How about D&D. Death and Dollars."

"That's lame," says Tank.

I quickly dash out all suggestions of a name for our team. "Na, no names. No chains or tats flauntin' our affiliation with one another. That's how the feds link cliques together. And that's how other squads know who to hit back at. We're gonna move in silence."

101

Shorty Got a Thug

"Hit niggas and they won't even know who's crushin' 'em or why," Silk jumps in without allowing me to complete my thoughts.

I make eye contact with him then take back control of the speech. "We're moving in complete silence. No flossing, clubbing—none of that shit. But we're knocking off heads, real efficiently. No drive-bys or other reckless hits. Every muthafucka we crush, we're gonna get right up on 'em and smash that ass."

"And leave no witnesses," infers Silk again.

I nod in agreement.

"I told ya'll the other day which niggas we're eliminating. If any other names need be added to that list in order for us to lock shit down, don't even mention their names to me. Just go out and crush 'em," I instruct.

Then I stand up and peer into the eyes of each member of my team, one by one. "I'ma head this family. And my word is not to be challenged." I pull my banger from my waist and hand it to Silk first. I say, "If you don't have complete loyalty to me, go ahead and pull the trigger now. Go ahead and take my life. Because if you violate later, I'm not gonna hesitate to take yours."

Ca$h

Silk sits the Glock back down on the table and smiles at my "G". I go to each member individually and give them the same opportunity.

My head is still intact which means no one pulled the trigger.

I say, "Each one of you just vowed loyalty to me. So from here on it's one hunnid or death. *La familia*. Now let's get our weight up!"

Leaving the meeting, I call my favorite girl as I head towards I-20.

"Hey shorty" is what I utter when Ni answers her phone.

"Brazen, why are you calling me? Don't you have Carmen?"

"I want to see you, it's very important."

"No! I have nothing to say to you. Please leave me alone, you are nothing but heartache."

"Listen shorty. I'm about to do something that may cost me my life if I fail. I just wanna see you one last time in case things don't turn out as planned. Fa real, Ni."

Shorty Got a Thug

"Brazen, you are not going to die. And I am not falling for any of your games. Go see Carmen! Maybe the two of you will perish together."

"Shorty you don't mean that."

Ni doesn't hear my last remark because she has hung up the phone.

CHAPTER 26

NIESHA

Thirty minutes after I hang up on Brazen, he's ringing my doorbell. I snatch open the door and fume, "What do you want?"

He looks at me with puppy dog eyes; a look he rarely inflects. He replies, "I told you I just wanna spend a little time with you." His voice is low and sincere. "What, a nigga ain't in your heart no more? I always thought our love was unconditional."

"Uggghhhh!" I scream out in exasperation. Then I step aside and let him come in.

"Damn, Ni, you're lookin' good," he compliments before making himself at home on the couch.

"I have on pajamas Brazen, but what—eva."

"Baby, you look good to *me*. That's all I'm saying. Is that okay with you?" he ask with puppy dog eyes.

I don't offer any response this time. I sit down on the couch next to him and my leg accidently brushes up against his as I'm folding my legs up under me, Indian style. Just that brief contact sends flutters throughout my body. But ain't no messy sheets type thing going on tonight. I scoot away a bit so that he gets the message.

Brazen shakes his head in amusement, like he wants to ask, "What's up with that?"

What he actually says is "I feel ya, baby. Trust, I didn't come over here on no booty call type shit. My love for you runs way deeper than a nut."

I suck my teeth.

"Tell that to someone who'll believe it. You gave up what we had for a nut. Or has Carmen become much more to you now?" I sling my words like a baseball bat. I swear if I could, I would kick his ass every time I think about him and her together.

"Ni, I already explained that to you," Brazen says softly, "I didn't come here to fight. I came to tell you that I'm about to reach for the sky. I'ma either get rich or get killed. Baby, I know you don't agree with how I'm going about it but try to believe that it's all gonna work out." He places a hand on one of mine, which are folded in my lap.

"Boy, you sound stupid." I snatch my hands from under his and a look of disappointment registers on his face.

"Maybe I am," he allows. "Anyway, I came to give you something." Brazen pulls out a large diamond engagement ring. He gently slides it onto my ring finger. "Neva take that off, Dark Cream. I'ma come back for you, I promise." The emotion in his voice is thick.

I get emotional myself. With tears running down my face, I say, "I can't do this, Brazen. Please! If you truly love me just let me go."

I take the ring off and try to press it into the palm of his hand.

Brazen closes his hand so that I can't force the ring into it. "I could never let you go, Ni. Not ever, baby," he vows. Then he takes the ring and puts it back on my finger.

I start to protest but he puts a finger to his mouth. "Shh! Don't say anything. Just let me hold you."

When his arms go around me, I stiffen. Then my resolve weakens and I melt into his arms. I quickly ask God to give me the strength to fight off the longing in my heart.

I feel stronger instantly.

Shorty Got a Thug

I extract myself from Brazen's arms and push away. I look into his eye and tell him, "I don't want you to hold me—ever again."

Brazen lets out a long breath.

"Damn that hurts. But I know that's not your heart talking," he reads me.

Whole minutes pass in silence.

Then, "Ni let me ask you something. What happened that night before you got arrested?"

"I'd prefer not to talk about it." I drop my head and reply.

But just that little inquiry causes me to re-live the whole horrible assault. I break down.

Brazen takes me in his arms and rocks me. After a while, my sobs turn into sniffling. Eventually I stop crying, and that's when I tell Brazen exactly what Tori did to me.

Brazen's tears wet his face and his jaws begin to twitch. A thick vein near his temple pulsates.

"I'ma handle it, Ni. Trust and believe that nigga will never stand trial," he vows.

I look at him, understanding him clearly. "No Brazen," I say.

108

Ca$h

But I know that he's gonna carry out his threat.so all I can do is ask God to forgive me for telling Brazen what Tori did to me.

I should have known better.

CHAPTER 27
Brazen

My team is moving work like crazy. So, of course, other niggas are feeling some kinda way since we're eating good and they're eating less. Dee dropped some product with a few of her trap stars on the Westside and some fools from Nawlins caught feelings because our product is superior and it cut into their sales. Without any words being passed they strapped up and crushed one of Dee's workers. Like we're gonna bow down.

"Them niggas think they runnin' something in my city? Ok! I'ma do 'em much worse than Katrina did." I spazz

"Brazen, just calm down and let me handle it. Trust, I'm already on it," Dee says.

I let out a deep sigh. "Handle it then. But don't forget to move in silence. Take Unc and Tank with you," I instruct her.

The look on her face chastises me for questioning her gangsta. I say, "Dee, I know you're official with ya murder game, and Butta is too. But appease my nerves, a'ight?"

Dee nods her head; we touch fists and part ways.

An hour after leaving the apartment complex near Hightower, where I spoke with Dee, I'm behind the wheel of a hooptie with Silk riding shotgun.

"Who is this nigga we're about to smash? I hope it's an *ese* or one of those fools from Nawlins," Silk says hopefully. His appetite for crushing both factors is almost unquenchable.

Silk is fingering his fo-fo.

"Nah, fam, this one is personal. This bitch ass nigga violated in the worst way," I say over the lyrics of Big Sean that's beatin' in the car.

"Violated how?" he ask.

"Neva mind all that just hold me down," I reply sternly.

"Hold up, homie," rejects Silk. "You my nigga, and I understand you the HNIC, but you can't be handling me like I sit down to pee."

"Bruh, you talkin' 'bout anything?"

"I'm just letting you know," he states.

Shorty Got a Thug

"Damn, let me find out you're one of those sensitive thugs." I crack, diffusing what could have been a real confrontation.

"Is *you* saying anything?" Silk says much too late because now we've just pulled up behind the silver Lexus Coupe that I know belongs to my prey.

For some strange reason I caught hell talking Carmen into setting this nigga up for me. But stiff dick and persistence broke her down.

We have to lay in wait two hours before Tori comes out of the restaurant where he's been dining with Carmen. She exits two steps ahead of him. As planned Carmen gets in her own car and goes on about her business.

I follow Tori from Riverdale Road to Camp Creek Parkway where he lives, without the fool realizing that I am on that ass. As soon as he pulls into his driveway and gets out of his whip, me and my nigga hop out the hooptie and converge on him.

Staring at the hot end of our bangers, Tori screams like he's wearing a thong underneath his slacks. I crack him over the head with my four-fifth and he crumples to the ground, whimpering.

"Shut yo bitch ass up!" I bark.

"Please don't hurt me. What do you want? I don't have any cash on me."

Boc! That's the clap of Silk's fo-fo.

Tori grabs his stomach and winces. I grab a hold of his collar and push my banger in his mouth. "You like raping women, huh? Well, Ni says hello!"

Bok! Bok!

That's the sound of murder.

CHAPTER 28
Niesha

A loud banging on my door jolts me out of my sleep much earlier than I planned to wake up this Saturday morning. I pull on some sweats and an oversized t-shirt and hurry to the door thinking it's Brazen and he's in some type of trouble.

I look through the peep hole and there's two middle age black men standing outside my door. I make them out to be cops. I guess ten years of dealing with Brazen and all of his run-ins with the law has made me keenly aware of po-po. These two outside my door aren't in uniform but they smell like cops.

As soon as I open the door they hold up their gold shields. The shorter of the two takes command. "Are you Niesha Smiley?" he asks.

"Yes I am."

"I'm Detective Brown and this is Detective Whatley. If we can step inside we'd like to ask you a few questions. "

"Concerning what?"

"May we come inside?"

"Of course." I step aside and allow them to enter. My mind is racing. *Is Brazen in trouble or perhaps dead?*

I'm seated on my living room couch next to Brown and across from Whatley who's seated in my silk covered chair.

"Did you know Tori Atkinson?" begins Brown.

"Yes," I answer honestly while trying to guess what this is in regards to.

"How did you know him?"

"Detective Brown, since you're here asking me about him I'm sure you are aware of my acquaintance with Mr. Atkinson. Are you here on behalf of the prosecutor's office, concerning the assault Mr. Atkinson committed against me?" I delve.

"No. We're here to ask if you know anything about the murder of Mr. Atkinson who was shot to death last night. You wouldn't have anything to do with that, would you?"

If I weren't already seated the news would have knocked me off my feet.

"No, of course not," I manage to respond to the detective's questions. "Can you tell me what happened?"

Shorty Got a Thug

The detectives take turns telling me how Tori was gunned down and murdered in the driveway of his home. Immediately I know that Brazen had something to do with it, and that anything I say could possibly point the detectives in his direction. Of course, I would never do that. I always have and always will protect Brazen.

I say to the detectives, "Due to the seriousness of your inquiry, I believe it would be in my best interest not to answer anymore of your questions until I have consulted with an attorney."

Both detectives look at me as if surprised by my response. Brown says, "You're not a suspect at this point, so what's your concern?"

"Detective, I'm going to call my attorney now." I reach for my cordless phone on the end table.

Brown abruptly stands then so does Whatley. "We'll be seeing you again," threatens Brown.

As soon as they are gone, with trembling hands I hurriedly call Brazen.

CHAPTER 29
BRAZEN

"Calm down Ni, it ain't all that serious. Niggas get they shit pushed back er'day of the week. Dude just got what was coming to him because that's the law of the land," I respond after listening to Ni tell me what the detectives said to her.

I'm careful not to say anything that would implicate me in Tori's murder, just on the slight chance that Ni's phone has been bugged. Not likely, because it's too soon after the murder. But, better safe than sorry.

I'm sure Ni knows that I bodied that nigga, and knowing Ni like I do, I'm sure she feels somewhat responsible for dude gettin' crushed. Ni wanted me to fall back and let the courts handle dude. Neva eva dat! Niggas touch mine I'ma deal with that ass swift and with finality. Fuckin' with shorty will get a nigga's thoughts sprayed out on the pavement.

Shorty Got a Thug

I can sense that Ni is nervous about the detectives having questioned her. So I dip by her house to try to ease her worries.

As soon as I'm inside her house and chilling she says, "I feel terrible. Yes, Tori deserved to be punished for forcing himself on me but only God has the right to take a person's life. I feel so guilty."

Tears fall from her eyes and wet her shirt.

I pull her into my arms and let her cry against my chest. "God won't hold you accountable for what *I* did. That's my cross to bear," I try to convince her.

It takes hours for me to get Ni's mind right. In the meantime I get a text from Dee that requires immediate attention, so I tell Ni that I gotta bounce. Before I leave, I try to hand her five racks. "This is just a li'l something to help you out," I say.

Ni snatches her hand back like I'm tryna hand her a ticking bomb. "No, thank you! I know where that came from." She turns her nose up at my drug money.

I shake my head and laugh.

"Yeah, now I'm convinced that you need to be committed. Girl, black folks don't turn down money."

Ca$h

"Shut up, Brazen," she replies, playfully punching me in the shoulder.

"I'm fa real, shorty. Girl, you're throwed off. Yo, close your eyes, let me get that piece of lint off of those long ass eye lashes before it gets in your eye."

"Okay, but be careful, don't poke me in the eye," says shorty, closing her eyes and standing very still.

There's no lint on her eye lashes. I smile at my juvenile tactic because it worked. Quickly I lean forward and press my lips against Ni's.

I'm up and out the door before Ni can protest.

A couple of days later I send Ni to retain an attorney so that further inquiries from homicide detectives will have to go through the lawyer. I know that Ni is official—I trained her properly—but I still didn't want po-po pressing her.

With that handled my attention is turned back to business. My team has crushed the Nawlins dudes who got at us first.

"Tell me how it went down," I say to Dee. The whole squad is present at the house where we meet to discuss business and such.

119

Shorty Got a Thug

Dee reports, "Tank and Unc smashed two of them niggas coming out of a sports bar on Moreland Ave. I rocked another one of them to sleep last night sitting outside his baby mama's crib. Crept that nigga real sweet. Left him nodded on the steering wheel of his whip, no witnesses. Butta and this young nigga off James P. Brawley took out DeVante."

"DeVante? You talking about the tall nigga with the long dreads, who drives that black Denali?" I ask.

"Yep, he was the one who sent them niggas at our workers," reports Tank.

"Who is the young nigga who rode out on the hit with Butta?" I direct the question to Dee.

"You know Quis; he's the one with those mix tapes out. Baby boy's murder game is as sick as his rap game. All I did was lead DeVante to a certain spot, from there Quis did all the work. I'm telling you, Brazen, that young nigga is the truth," Butta sings his praises.

I peep Dee's expression change. She's jealous for some reason.

"Youngin is official," co-signs Silk, which carries weight with me.

"Hit Marquis up and tell him to come out here. I'ma move him up in rank. Let him control that whole area, him

120

and Butta. Dee, I'ma pull you off the streets. From now on you're strictly distribution and head knockin'. I'ma do that because you been fuckin' with the game for years and your face is known by po-po," I explain.

"But, Brazen, you know I'm street. I like to be out there with the street team," she objects, but I'm not hearing it.

"I feel you but my decision is final."

Butta hit Marquis up. Forty minutes later he's in a seat at the table with the rest of us. I let him know that I'm hearing good things about his gangsta and I like the way he handled that recent thing with DeVante.

"So, I'm promoting you," I say, patting him on the back in a congratulatory manner.

After defining his role to him I pull the youngin to the side and give him a warning. "Youngin," I say in a no-nonsense tone as I look him in the eye. "Butta is a bad bitch. She's so bad, sometimes I look at her and wanna fuck her myself. But I remind myself that she's forbidden fruit because she belongs to Dee. What I'm saying is—you can't cross that line. Do you understand me?" My eyes do not blink.

Shorty Got a Thug

Marquis needs to know that he can't take it there, ever. And if he does, I'ma be his executioner. I tell him exactly that. "Ain't no pussy worth your life," I reiterate.

"I understand you fully, fam," he says.

"Please do." I hold out my fist.

Marquis touches his fists to mine.

"Loyalty or death," vows Marquis.

*****

After the meeting Fat Cat is rolling with me as I make a few drops. I handle my business then I take my dude home. At Fat Cat's crib I go inside for a minute to check out a rack of guns he came across earlier in the week.

Sitting in the den of Fat Cat's condo I examine a couple choppers, a half dozen Glock .40s, an AR-15 and a fo-fifth. "What was the ticket on all of this?" I ask out of curiosity.

When Fat Cat responds I let out a low whistle.

Just then Fat Cat's girl Shanteria prances into the room in skin-toned boy shorts and a tee-shirt so thin her nipples greet a nigga before her smile does. "Oh, heyyy Brazen. What's up, bro?" She flashes me an extra big smile.

Ca$h

Shanteria is a pretty ass bitch, no doubt. She's about 5'5" and sexy as hell. Like Kanye said, she had an ass that would swallow up a g-string and up top two bee stings. Plus she's cute and she knows it. Still she ain't nothing but a rat who is after my nigga's cheese. But my nigga is blind to her shit.

Shanteria is from VA. I figure the bitch moved to the 'A' because niggas back in her hometown Norfolk had already ran through her and was no longer willing to drop stacks in the lap of a two dollar trick.

"Sup, Shanteria," I respond dryly.

She gets all up in my space, fingering the chain that I'm rockin'. "Ooh! I like this," she purrs, nipples against my chest.

"Girl, go put on some clothes! Don't you see I got company?" Fat Cat tries to check her.

"Aww, boo, Brazen is family," Shanteria dismisses him.

Fat Cat has to get stupid to make her obey him. Shanteria leaves out of the den in a huff.

"Dawg, I hate to be the one to tell you but you ain't got yourself nothing in that one. Work on replacing her before she knows too much," I advise Fat Cat.

"Nah, fam, you're wrong about baby girl, she's a rider," he defends the scut bucket ass ho.

"A rider?" I grit. "Bruh, that bitch ain't no more a rider than I'm the Prophet Muhammad. I'm warning you, fam. I'll murk you before I allow you to let a bitch bring us all down. Ain't nobody getting in the way of my check."

Fat Cat looks at me like he's feelin' some kinda way, but he doesn't verbalize what's on his mind. If the fat ass nigga could see past his dick he would peep that his girl ain't nothing to hold onto.

I toss him a grip and grab the fo-fifth and two of the Glocks out of his cache.

I'ma holla," I say, headed for the door.

"Bye, Brazen," Shanteria calls out from the hallway.

I look at her with my coldest stare.

Bitch if your ass was on fire I wouldn't piss on you.

CHAPTER 30
<u>FAT CAT</u>

As soon as Brazen bounces I storm up to Shanteria and snatch her by her $800 weave. "Why the fuck was you all up in my people's face, like you some groupie bitch?"

"Pssst! Wasn't nobody all up in his face. You sound stupid!" she shoots back, being disrespectful.

"Yeah the fuck you were. And you need to watch ya slick mouth before you make me slap you in it," I say, still holding her by her hair.

"Let me go muthafucka! Aww! You're hurting me, shit!" she cries.

I let her go but I'm still heated.

"You act like you wanna get with Brazen." I toss that out there to see how Shanteria responds.

Straight up, I've always felt like she wanted my nigga because she was always asking me shit about him. Now she's saying, "Maybe I should've got with Brazen instead of your insecure ass. Step ya game up and you won't be shook by Brazen's swag."

125

Shorty Got a Thug

Before I know it Shanteria is on her ass and I'm staring at my hand, like what happened?

Shanteria jumps up and claws my face like a hell cat. The next thing I know I've knocked her unconscious.

Damn!

CHAPTER 31

Brazen

This is the dumb shit that I was talking about. Fat Cat is locked up for domestic violence and that gutter snipe bitch of his is laid up in Piedmont Hospital with a fractured jaw and a concussion.

On my team, I would've smashed that bitch a long time ago, if I was Fat Cat. I most definitely would've got in that ass last night for the total disrespect she showed towards him when I fell through there.

Of course I never would've had that nothing ass bitch playing wifey in the first place. I'm pissed because me and the others on the team are tryna get to this check, and Fat Cat is locked up over a chicken box bitch.

"Let his stupid ass sit in jail for a week or so, that'll teach him about fucking with that poison ass ho," Silk suggests.

"Yeah, that's just what I'ma do." I decide as I relax in the passenger seat of Silk's metallic silver Dodge Charger while we cruise the city checking our spots.

Shorty Got a Thug

A week later Dee reminds me that I'm supposed to bail Fat Cat out of jail. "You want me to go handle it?" she offers.

I think it over for a minute, deciding against it. "Nah, I don't want any of our names connected to each other. I'll have Carmen handle it," I decide.

I hit Carmen up and give her the instructions on how she is supposed to bond Fat Cat out of jail. "Use some of the money that's in those shoe boxes in your closet," I tell her.

"Ok, daddy, is there a chance I will see you today? My oil needs changing." She's fiending for the dick.

I don't really wanna fuck with Carmen outside of business no more because every time I run up in her I feel real fucked up over how I'm playing Ni. But the dick controls Carmen more than the duckets do so I'ma continue to smash her until I no longer need her services. "I'ma fall through there later," I half promise.

A short while later I'm with Unc, Tank and Silk choppin' it up about Fat Cat. Unc says, "Pussy befalls a hustla more often than anything."

"True," I agree. "Fat Cat gon' have to make a choice."

Ca$h

I discuss other business with my mans, particularly the hit they're planning on some Mexican niggas, who are affiliated with the vicious M-13 gang. I listen to Silk detail how they plan to crush a few eses out in Gwinnett.

"It'll have double benefit to us. One, these niggas just took some of our clientele and I want it back. Secondly, when we get at 'em I expect them to have a lot of work up in that spot," Silk predicts.

"And a lot of protection, too," I toss back.

"But we can get up on 'em before they know what hit 'em," says Tank.

I look at Unc. "What you think?" I ask.

"It can be done," he replies but not with the confidence I need to hear. So my decision is made.

"Ya'll hold off on that until I can strap up with ya'll. And when we go at 'em we're taking the whole team. Plus, six bodies is gonna hit the news and bring heat. So let's sit on that for a minute," I say.

Silk gets the screw face.

I ignore him for now. I touch fists wit' my niggas then bounce.

Leaving Silk's spot I head to Atlanta Medical Center. I'm just in time to catch Ni down in the cafeteria. I walk up behind my Dark Cream and cover her eyes.

129

Shorty Got a Thug

I whisper on her neck, "Guess who's joining you for lunch."

"Um, my baby, T-Pain."

"Nah."

"My honey Blair Underwood." She giggles.

"One more wrong guess and I'ma bite your ear lobe off."

"Ohhh, it must be my sweetest weakness—this man named Brazen."

I remove my hands from over her eyes and she turns around wearing a pretty smile. "Brazen, what are you doing here?"

The light admonishment can't hide the happiness I hear in her voice.

130

CHAPTER 32
NIESHA

The smell of Prada cologne on Brazen intoxicates my senses for a moment. He knows that I absolutely love that scent because I always purchased Prada cologne for him.

Holding my tray with both hands I look into his eyes and my heart skips like a six-year old girl's might on Christmas Eve. I feel so weak for Brazen.

"I ask what you are doing here." I manage to repeat.

"I wanted to eat lunch with my girl. Anything wrong with that?" He takes the tray out of my hand and I follow him to a vacant table. After sitting the tray down, Brazen pulls out my chair for me. Then he bends and kisses me on the cheek before sitting across from me.

"What's that you're eating?" he ask.

"Crab and shrimp salad. It's really good, would you like to try some?" I hold out a forkful to him.

"Nah, what I wanna eat ain't on that fork," he responds, licking his lips.

"You're nasty," I chuckle.

"But you love it." He takes the fork and begins feeding me like I'm two years old. It's a tender moment that defies the thug that he is.

Damn I love him so much.

"Ni, you know I love you right?" Brazen says, breaking my daydream.

"Do you?"

"Yes, I do."

"But not as much as you love the streets." I frown.

"That's not true, shorty. It's just that the streets is the only way I know to get what I need," he lamely suggest.

I just shake my head as he continues.

"Ni, I got dreams and goals, and you're a part of all of 'em. I told you before, I wouldn't feel like a man if I couldn't provide you with everything you deserve and desire."

I begin to respond but he hushes me with a gesture of his hand. "Finish eating, baby girl. Just use that pretty mouth to chew with, I'll do all the talking."

Ca$h

By the time lunch is over and Brazen walks me back to my unit, my head is spinning. Love songs play in my mind and his scent remains with me the rest of the day.

At home I call up my mom. She listens nonjudgmentally as I replay Brazen's words.

"Well, he's not making it easy for you," she teases.

"I know right?" I sigh heavily as I rub my forehead.

My phone beeps with a call from Carmen. I ask my mother to hold on while I answer the other line.

"Why are you calling me?" I snap.

"To let you know that I'm carrying Brazen's child," she discloses with pleasure.

My heart crumbles into a thousand broken pieces and it's hard to breathe.

CHAPTER 33

Brazen

"What the fuck you mean you pregnant?" I scream as if Carmen has just told me that she has the HIV virus.

"Well damn! Do you have to yell in my face?" She plops down on her bed and pokes her lips out.

"Bitch, I ought to spit in yo face. I know you're on some thirsty ass shit, tryna baby trap a nigga!" I'm pacing the room, fists clenched so tight my hands feel numb.

What the fuck was I thinkin' when I ran up in this trick raw? And, how long ago was that? I gotta think back because Carmen is a real slick bitch.

"Can't you at least *pretend* to be happy? Just think, I may give you a little Junior." The smirk on her face inflames me more.

"It's not happening, bitch." I toss a rack on the bed. "Handle your business."

Ca$h

Carmen slaps the money onto the floor. "I'm not having an abortion!"

"By choice or by force. You decide." I stop pacing and stand in front of her sneering.

"Or what?" she challenges me.

"Trust, you don't want me to answer that. Your ass is on some drama shit, that's why you called Ni with the news first." I point my finger in her face and add, "You better fall back off of shorty with that dumb shit. You hear me?"

Tears drip from her eyes as she nods her head up and down.

Fuck Carmen's tears, they don't mean shit to me. I give her one last cold look and I bounce.

Now I'm cruising I-285 with Fat Cat in the truck with me. This is the first time I've kicked it with him since he was bonded out of jail a few days ago. I put it to him in the raw, no chaser. "Fam, you see how you got locked up behind some unnecessary shit with Shanteria? What if popo had found all those guns up in your spot? Nigga, you would be headed to the feds and heat would be on the whole team."

"I feel you bruh, but my girl didn't call 911, a neighbor did." He defends her.

135

Shorty Got a Thug

"Same result. The ho is trouble, get rid of her." I slide him a fo-fifth and he snatches his hand away.

"You gotta do it, homie. She knows too much," I speak sternly.

"Bruh, don't make me do my girl, I love shorty."

I tuck the burner back in my waist. "A'ight, nigga, but you bet' not let nothing else like this happen," I warn him.

"I won't," he promises while visibly breathing a sigh of relief.

We exit I-285 on Bankhead Highway and pull into a gas station. I put the burner under the seat and hop out to go pay for a fill up. Heading back to my truck I see two dudes who I recognize instantly. Both are Juvie's li'l cousins.

"Sup? One of 'em nods and smiles at me but I sense beef.

"I heard it was you who killed my cousin," accuses the other, stepping closer to me, burner in hand.

I reach for my fo-fifth but of course it's in the truck.

I see the little nigga's hand come up gripping steel. The burner barks loud and vengefully.

136

Ca$h
Hot lead fills my body, slumping me to the ground.

CHAPTER 34

Dee

"Why the fuck did you leave him?"

I'm all in Fat Cat's face ready for whatever. We're in the waiting room of the ER but it don't even matter. This fat ass coward can get it right here, right now.

"I had to drive off when the police arrived because Brazen had burners in the truck and they might have bodies on them," Fat Cat explains lamely.

"Fool, you could've just tossed the guns. You don't leave him leaking on the ground! And why you ain't bust one of the niggas who wet him?" I snarl.

"Bitch, you questioning my G?" he has the muthafuckin' audacity to ask.

"What G? Nigga, you acting like you got a P!" I check him.

Fat Cat snatches me by my sweater and chokes me.

Butta steps up and shoves her banger in his side. "Don't get put in a shit bag."

"Y'all chill!" barks Silk. He quickly glances around to see if security has been alerted by the commotion.

Ca$h

"Later for you, nigga," I scoff at Fat Cat when he releases me.

Tempers flare up again when Fat Cat threatens Butta. My boo is about to wet him up but Marquis drags her outside.

As if all of this isn't enough, Carmen comes flying into the ER screaming, "Lawd please don't let my hubby be dead! Somebody take me to him. If he dies I wanna die too!"

Niesha springs up out of her chair and snatches Carmen by the arm. "Heifer, if you don't sit your ass down somewhere I swear I'm going to beat you silly," she grits.

Carmen pulls away and darts behind Tank.

"Any place, any time," she says, peeking out from behind Tank's massive frame, frontin'.

Nobody says anything after that but the tension in the ER is thick. I eye Fat Cat, tryna bait him into his own funeral. But he knows that I'm not the average bitch. I let them thangs pop. Fat Cat is just a hustla, I'm a hustla and a killa. And over Brazen I'll kill fast.

"You got something on your mind?" I can't help but challenge Fat Cat.

He says nothing.

Now tell me who's the bitch? I say to myself, leaning back in the hard plastic seat and letting out a

139

frustrated breath. I bite my nails worrying whether or not Brazen is gonna make it. If he dies I'm murking Fat Cat right here in the ER. No lie.

I love Brazen, not on no sexual tip because I don't do dick. I love that nigga like a brother because he's real wit his shit. And he treats me with the same respect he has for the men on our team. It don't matter to Brazen that I'm a stud, all that matters to him is I'm official. I appreciate that.

In fact Silk is the only nigga on the team who doesn't respect how I get down. He swears that I hate men but that's not the case. "A dude must've molested you growing up." Silk once assumed incorrectly, tryna stereotype me.

I didn't even respond because all he needs to know is that I ride hard for the team. The truth is I have never had any dick, never wanted any after I got my first taste of pussy.

I was a thirteen year old tomboy who hustled on the block with all the dudes. I wasn't nothing close to eye candy so they weren't sweating me too close. I pitched stones and smoked weed with them all day and night, and I even had a secret crush on one hard head.

Who I really had a thing for was Jasmine. Jasmine was this bad ass red bone chick that lived in the apartment complex on Maynard Drive where I hustled. I would watch Jasmine come and go, and I swear she was the baddest bitch to ever put on a pair of heels. All of the drug dealers were checkin' for Jasmine but she was very selective about the niggas she fucked with. She wasn't a jump-off.

I was still a virgin in every way, and I can't even say I thought about Jasmine sexually. I just dug that bitch's style, straight up. One night I was on my way home from the trap when I heard, "Dee, come here for a minute." I went up to Jasmine's front door and she invited me inside.

"Why are you looking at me like that? You're always staring at me," she observed.

"I'm—sorry." My eyes went straight to the floor.

With a finger Jasmine tilted my head up and kissed me softly. Instinctively I pushed my tongue into her mouth and wrapped it around hers. Her mouth tasted so good it was dizzying. I wanted to suck her tongue forever.

When the kiss ended Jasmine led me into her bedroom by the hand and we kissed again at the foot of her bed. "Undress me. Don't you want to see what I look like naked?" she asked.

I was too nervous to speak so I simply nodded my head. Jasmine held her arms above her head as I removed

141

her baby t-shirt. She was braless underneath. Her golden brown titties made me swallow. They were beautiful, and tapered down to her flat tummy. "Kiss my titties, Dee." Her voice was hypnotizing.

I no longer had a will of my own. I was moving to the command of Jasmine's seductive voice and my own mounting desire. Her brown nipples were succulent in my mouth. I sucked one and then the other as tenderly as my inexperience would allow. Jasmine's hands were in my hair and as I sucked those lovely nipples I inhaled the feminine fragrance of her body. Without being instructed I slid her black leggings off.

"Feel my pussy, Dee," she said, taking my hand and placing it between her thighs.

Jasmine's pussy was bald and as plump as a Georgia peach. It took my whole hand to cup it. And it was so wet.

She eased down on the bed and told me to undress. I stood stock still, ashamed to take my clothes off and expose my nakedness to Jasmine. What I had underneath my Levi's and hoodie could not compare to Jasmine's assets.

Being ten years older than me Jasmine must've sensed my insecurity about my body. She sat up and without saying a word helped me out of my clothes.

Ca$h

Like a shy little girl I covered my small breasts with my arms while sucking in my stomach. I was ashamed of my plumpness.

Jasmine said, "Every girl and woman is beautiful in her own way." Then she removed my arms from over my little buds and covered one of them with her mouth. It felt better than counting money.

When Jasmine's hand eased between my thighs and rubbed my pussy my legs began to shake. She brought her hand up to her mouth and licked my virgin juices off of her fingers. My pussy throbbed and my clit jumped. I wanted to taste her.

"Talk to me, Dee. Don't be shy, you gotta be as confident now as you are when you're out there grindin'. C'mon, tell me what you wanna do to me," prodded Jasmine.

The words came out of my mouth on their own accord. "I wanna kiss you down there," I mumbled.

"No, baby, that's not gonna get it, you gotta say it. C'mon, tell me so I can get turned on," encouraged Jasmine.

"Ok. I wanna eat—your pussy." My eyes stared at the floor.

Shorty Got a Thug

"Really?" she asked. "Well, do you know what a clit is?"

I looked up and nodded my head. I had overheard an older cousin of mine talking about playing with her clit. I tried it and got hooked on it. For the past six months I had been masturbating almost every night. So, not only did I know what a clit was, I also knew how to pop a pussy.

"Come taste this pretty pink pussy, Dee," cooed Jasmine. She gently opened her meaty lips and showed me her glistening pinkness. I dove in head first. And from that moment on, I was gone off that twat.

Jasmine got my head a few times then lost interest. Me, I was in love! Every time I would see a nigga come over to visit her I would shoot up her apartment. When Jasmine moved away I was sick. Although I had plenty girlfriends after Jasmine, I never got over her until I met Butta.

My mind comes back to the present, and once again my eyes lock with Fat Cat's. I break my stare only because I have to go check on Butta, she has been outside with Marquis way too long.

144

CHAPTER 35

Brazen

Those lil niggas tried to crush me. Man, I was slippin' bad, but never again—I put that on my love for Ni! They fucked up when they didn't kill me, now they're about to see how a real killa gets down.

It's been a week since I got shot. I took a slug in the side, one in the hip, another grazed my face. But it's all good, I'm out of the ICU and in a private room, plotting revenge.

Ni walks in looking all good in a thin summer dress that shows off the contours of her figure without advertising sex. "Good afternoon, Brazen. How are you feeling today?" she ask.

"A little weak still but I'm not complaining, at least I'm still alive," I say.

"Praise the Almighty," replies Ni taking a seat in the chair close to the bed. "I don't know what I would've done if…" she allows the thought to go unspoken but I comprehend.

Shorty Got a Thug

"Shorty, ain't nothing gonna happen like that," I discount her fears.

"It almost did."

"Yeah but *almost* doesn't count. I promise to be more careful from now on."

"Please do." She leans over and kisses me.

"Yeah, you love me for sure, I see that." I flash her a little smile letting her know that I appreciate her.

"Of course I do, though I don't know why."

"You love me because I got that thug in me," I boast.

"I do not!"

"No? Well, why you kiss me and my breath is still crusty and shit?"

Ni laughs and replies, "Brazen, you're so silly. Please tell me you've brushed your teeth."

"Nope. Not in two days. My mouth probably smelling like skunk booty and you're lovin' it," I tease her.

"Eww!" Ni pounces right up and goes into the bathroom, returning with toothbrush, toothpaste, and a water pan.

I slaughter the monster that is my breath. Now that I'm Colgate fresh Ni gives me another kiss. The sound of someone clearing their throat interrupts us.

Ca$h

From the doorway Carmen says, "I'm gonna pretend I didn't see that."

Ni's head snaps in that direction. "Or else?" she remarks.

"Or I might act a donkey."

"Please do. I'm itching to kick off in your ass again." Ni gets up in Carmen's face.

"You know I'm pregnant with Brazen's child, if you hit me I'll press charges," Carmen hurries to say while taking a few steps backwards.

"I don't give a hot shit! Trick, I will beat that baby out of you!" snaps Ni who's becoming a real tigress.

I cut in before the fists begin flying. "Carmen, why don't you go down to the cafeteria and grab yourself something to eat?"

"I'm not hungry." Carmen replies defiantly.

"Well go watch other people eat."

"You're too funny." She humphs.

This bitch must take me for a joke.

"I tell you what, since you choose to act like a fucking child, I'ma treat you like one. Go stand over there in the corner with your nose against the wall and you bet' not move until I give you permission. Test my gangsta and watch how fast I get off in your ass!" Due

147

to my injuries my voice is as weak as my body but my tone is dead ass.

Carmen obeys me without a response.

"That's sad," interjects Ni, shaking her head. "Girl, do you have no backbone at all? No dang pride?"

"I'm not saying anything," utters Carmen from across the room in a corner.

My chest swells with arrogance. I know I'm that nigga. Ni sees the smirk on my face. She chops me down.

"I don't know why you're smiling, Brazen—like that makes you a boss. There's nothing cute about making a fool out of a woman. I can't stand her but disrespecting her does not impress me. You of all people should know that. If you disrespect her you you'll disrespect me."

"Nah, shorty I—"

"Save it, Brazen! I'm glad that you're okay but I won't be back to visit you; you do entirely too much for me. Take care, you and that pitiful fool over there deserve one another," scolds Ni then she storms out of the room.

My arrogance deflates like a punctured balloon.

"May I please come out of the corner now?" Carmen pleads.

Ca$h

"Yeah," I reply with reluctance.

Carmen sits on the side of my bed. She says, "Now you see that *that* bitch ain't a rider like me." She slides her hand inside my hospital gown and strokes my limp meat. It doesn't respond so Carmen replaces her hand with her mouth. A cough comes from the doorway.

"This is a hospital, not the VIP room of a strip club," admonishes a nurse.

Carmen rises up and sneers at the woman.

"Hater!"

CHAPTER 36

Niesha

I have said that I'm done with Brazen so many times and went back on my promise to myself, it's no wonder he takes me for granted. I mean, what reason does he have to fear losing me when I've accepted so much disrespect from him? What woman in her right mind allows her man to sleep around with her cousin and still love him?

Where they do that?

Brazen simply does not believe that I'm capable of letting him go. But this time I am truly done. Sooner or later a woman gets sick and tired of being sick and tired. After Brazen's shenanigans in that hospital room, I finally see him for what he is, a thug who has no respect for women. I am totally, absolutely, turned off.

It's been close to three months since I've seen or spoken to that man. I've changed my cell phone number and I do not answer the door when he comes ringing. I can't lie,

it's killing me to let go but a sistah has her game face on.
I'm determined to move on.

Presently I have a friend. His name is Omar and
he's thirty-eight years old, ten years older than me.
Omar kinda looks like the black novelist Eric Jerome
Dickey. Omar owns a small franchise of fitness centers
in the Southeast. He's a very ambitious and respectful
brother who has a vast knowledge of Black History. In
addition to being a successful entrepreneur, Omar is
street wise. He grew up in the notorious Vine City area
and was caught up in the streets before a tragedy
transformed him.

Omar's twin brother got killed right in front of him.
"After that, I owed it to his memory to change my life
around," he explained one day, sharing his past.

"That's refreshing to hear. So many brothers find it
impossible to effect change," I commented.

Omar and I talk often. We've gone out a few times
to dinner at various restaurants. We even went to church
together last Sunday. I enjoy his conversation as well as his
company but no, we have not become intimate. I am
definitely not ready to go there, Brazen is still too fresh in

my heart. I explained all of this to Omar and he says he understands.

Presently Omar and I are in my den playing Scrabble and sharing lemon pepper wings. Brazen would never play Scrabble, he would call it boring. The thought slips out of my mouth unintentionally.

"I'm sorry. I know you get tired of me bringing Brazen's name up, I'll try not to do it again." I apologize.

"Nah, it's understandable. I realize that he was a big part of your life so of course you relate everything to him."

His understanding is endearing.

"Niesha," he continues, "when we first met you told me that you are still in love with Brazen and that you aren't ready to become seriously involved with anyone new until he was completely out of your heart. So I'm going to be patient with you. I'm happy with the friendship that we have, for the moment."

"Thank you," I say. "Uh—can we finish this game another day?" referring to Scrabble.

"Why? Is it because I'm kicking your behind?" replies Omar teasingly.

"Nooooo! I would just prefer to watch a movie, if that's okay with you."

"It's fine," he says.

I pick the remote up off of my smoked black glass cocktail table and turn on the plasma television that's mounted on the wall while Omar browses through my DVDs. To my surprise he selects my favorite movie, *Love & Basketball.*

Halfway through the movie, my doorbell chimes. A co-worker of mine is supposed to come over and pick up her cell phone. She mistakenly left it at work and I brought it home to avoid putting her through the hassle of driving back to the job.

"Excuse me," I say to Omar. "Do you mind if I put the movie on pause while I answer the door?"

"No, not at all. Try not to get lost," he kids.

I promise not to.

The doorbell chimes over and over again as I search for my hand bag. I find it on the kitchen table. I get my co-workers phone out of the handbag and hurry to the door. "Dang, girl, I'm coming," I call out.

I open the front door and—*Oh lord!*

Shorty Got a Thug

CHAPTER 37

Brazen

I'm fully recovered from my injuries, but of course I'm left with battle scars and a hot thirst for revenge. The two youngins who tried to do me are, so far, hiding from what they can't duck forever. I won't rest until I crush both of 'em.

Me and my team are building our weight up, smashing any and everything that gets in our way. The bodies keep piling up; the streets don't have a clue as to who's behind the murders. We're moving in silence. Just the other night we did that thing that Silk had talked to me about months ago. We ran in on six M-13 affiliated Mexicans and left all of them flat-lined. Walked away with dumb, stupid work that they had up in their spot.

So far, my team has suffered no casualties, which is a blessing. Carmen is still making the runs for me to Miami, and no—the bitch didn't get an abortion. I wanna slump that bitch but I believe that if I do it while she's pregnant karma will serve me a cruel plate of payback.

Looks like I'm stuck with the ho becoming my baby's mama. I don't have no love for her and I haven't dicked the bitch in months. As long as she plays her role I'll continue to deal with her. As soon as her usefulness dries up or she begins to cause drama I'ma cancel the bitch.

I haven't talked to Ni in several months. I guess she has finally stopped loving a nigga. That's some hard shit to accept. Me and shorty got too much history between us to just let it go. Regardless to how I move, I love Ni. She's the only woman I truly want.

I'm on my way over to her house to find out what the business is. I pull up in front of her crib and spot a Dodge Ram parked behind her whip in the driveway. Don't tell me Ni has company.

My head pounds at the mere thought of that.

I lock and load one in the chamber of my new Ruger as I get out of my truck in a riff and hurry up to her door. I ring the muthafuckin' doorbell repeatedly. If Ni doesn't open this door soon I'ma do a kick door!

156

Ca$h

Just as I'm about to huff and puff and kick the fuckin' door in, Ni opens it. When she sees that it's me, her face looks like she's seen a ghost. "Brazen, what are you doing here? You can't pop up at my door any time you please!" she complains.

"Why not? You got something to hide?"

I brush right past her.

"You got a nigga up in here?" I ask over my shoulder.

"My voice is loud as I stalk towards the den, the logical place for Ni to entertain company.

"Ni runs up behind me and grabs my arm.

"Brazen, please don't start anything! We are not together anymore!" Her words twist my mouth into a hardened scowl.

"I want you to leave!" she shouts.

Her words bounce off my back as I snatch away from her and continue down the short hallway. I step into the den and see this older nigga lounging on the Italian leather sofa that I muthafuckin' bought.

Ni darts in front of me.

Dude says, "Niesha, is everything okay?"

I answer for her. "If it ain't, what you saying?" I raise my arm and point the Ruger dead between his eyes.

Ni is like a gnat, all in my face. "No, Brazen!" she pleads.

It only takes one hand to sling her little bitty ass out of the way. Homeboy stares at the Ruger and bows down to its threat. "Bruh, let's talk this out like men. Niesha and I are only friends," he begins but I cut him off.

"Nigga, I'm not your bruh! And if you know what's best for you, you would stay as far away from shorty as you can. Niesha belongs to me. Always has, always will. I'll kill or die to keep her. So until you're ready to go hard like that, I suggest you fall the fuck back."

I force the Ruger into the frightened dude's mouth and holding him by the collar I grit, "You see that pretty muthafucka right there?" I cut my eyes towards Ni.

Homeboy nods his recognition.

I say, "She don't need any friends. I'm her homie, her hubby, and her friend. And all of the above."

"Brazen, that's enough!" cries Ni. "You cannot control my life. Go tell Carmen who or who not to see!"

Ca$h

We shout back and forth until Ni finally wears me down. "Okay," I concede. "Fuck you! I'm out!" I spew, storming out of the den.

Parked down the street from Ni's house I have to wait thirty minutes before dude drives by in his Dodge Ram. Obviously he doesn't know what type of whip I'm pushing because I follow the fool all the way to a house out in Sandy Springs. As soon as he pulls into the driveway and slides out of his truck, I'm breathing on the back of his neck. "I told you I would kill to keep her, didn't I?" I remind him right before I prove it to him.

Carrying on as *brazen* as my name, I whip out my cell phone to snap a few pictures of dude lying in his driveway, crushed. I head straight to Ni's house and force her to go to a motel room with me.

"You cannot control me, Brazen! I'm tired of you!" She is kicking and fighting as I pull her into the room.

I pin her arms to her side and kiss her roughly. "You belong to me!" I say.

Ni bites my lip.

"Aww!" I yelp and push her down on the bed. Then I'm on top of her.

Shorty Got a Thug

Ni fights me but those jeans come off then her sweater. I pin her arms to the bed and exclaim, "Your body is so beautiful."

"Get off of me!" She struggles and squirms beneath my weight.

"I just wanna love you, Ni." I cover her breast with my mouth. My hand rubs her closely shaved pussy.

Ni fights a little longer but she can't resist this shit. I'm her addiction, just as she is mine. When I rub the swollen head of my dick up and down her moist slit, she begins to moan and grind up on me.

"Brazen, wrap up." She whispers into my shoulder.

I'm always strapped so that's not a problem. All I wanna do is make love to Ni and remind her that she's mine forever. Before the night is over she'll know that I go hard for her.

CHAPTER 38

Niesha

Brazen's thickness spreads me wide open. I scream out his name and dig my nails into his back. Inside my head it feels like I'm going crazy. I'm so angry with Brazen yet he's making me feel ooh so good.

"Oh—my—god, Brazen, you have my pussy on fiyah. Why do you do me like this? Get up!"

"Nah, shorty, I'ma make you come all over this big dick. Look down at it and watch it go in and out of you. Don't that shit turn you on?"

Brazen draws all the way out then pushes back in deeper. My head is lashing from side to side with so much pleasure there's no need to reply. This nigga still has me gone.

"Ni, why you have that nigga all up in your spot? Don't you know I will kill you if you ever gave my pussy away?" He's stroking in and out to the rhythm of his voice.

Shorty Got a Thug

"It's not your pussy Brazen, it belongs to me," I reply, throwing it back at him nevertheless.

"Bullshit! It's mine, you just carry it around. Ain't that right?"

"No," I answer defiantly, trying to hold on to something. I can't surrender everything to him.

"Well, if it ain't mines I'm wasting my time," counters Brazen and I feel him withdrawing himself from inside of me.

"Please don't take it out." I fall weak and beg. *I'm so pitiful!*

Brazen plunges back inside of me. He gets on his knees and throws one of my legs over his shoulder, gripping me by the ass with both hands. "Is this my pussy?" He plows hard.

"Yes baby, it's yours."

"This my ass too?"

"Ohhh yessss." I cry out and dig my nails into his back as he hits that spot.

"What about your titties, who do they belong to?"

"You Brazen, you." I pant. "Every part of me is yours. Even my toes."

"Do I fuck you good?" He has my feet up on his shoulders and his hands grip my ass.

162

Ca$h

"Yes—lawd!" My pussy is squishing.

"Turn around. Face down, ass in the air. Pop that pussy for me," he commands.

I'm under his spell. I pop it like a porn queen. Brazen enters me from behind and it feels sooooo damn good! "Smack my ass," I cry out.

Brazen smacks my ass, drives his dick inside me so deep I swear it's touching my brain. He pulls my hair and talks real dirty to me while dicking me half to death. I cum about a zillion times. Out of breath, I pant, "Come for me, baby."

"Can I take the condom off and bust a big ass nut all up inside this good pussy?"

"You can do whatever you want." *Now why did I say that?*

I feel Brazen pull out, then re-enter me raw. I'm about to tell him to put the condom back on when he covers my mouth with his and takes my senses again.

"Ohhhh, baby, your pussy is so wet and juicy," exclaims Brazen. "Work your muscles for me."

I work those bad boys like they are the hands of a masseuse. Brazen goes ape up in my kitty. I scream out his name and we explode together. I collapse on my stomach, blinking my eyes because I fear that I've just gone blind. "Brazen, I can't see." I whine.

He just laughs with arrogance to his tone. He knows that he handled the damn thing. "C'mere Ni, let me hold you." He pulls me into his arms and I rest my head on his chest and doze off into a beautiful dream.

The smell of weed awakens me. Brazen is up smoking a blunt of loud. Seeing that I'm awake he smiles and we say in unison to each other, "I love you."

"How much do you love me?" I ask him.

"Do you really want to know?" he replies, then studies my expression.

"Yes."

"Ok. Check this out." Brazen grabs his jeans off the floor and pulls out his cell phone. He scrolls through it then hands the phone to me. I stare at the screen in horror as I recognize Omar's truck.

"That's how much I love you," declares Brazen, pointing to Omar sprawled out on the ground on the screen.

I scramble out of bed, rush to the bathroom and fall to my knees at the toilet. I vomit so violently I can hardly breathe.

CHAPTER 39
Brazen

Ni ain't fuckin wit' me at all anymore after what I showed her on my phone a few weeks ago. I hear that popo is all over her, but I'm not worried about it, shorty would never flip. Quiet as it's kept, she's my backbone—fuck what I do. In the end I do it for the both of us.

Meanwhile my team is making it do what it do. We're getting it in duffel bags. It's not all gravy, though. Problems poppin' up left and right. Our spot on Glenwood Drive got jacked. A nigga bought two bricks from Fat Cat with counterfeit money. And Dee thinks Marquis is bangin' Butta.

Right now Silk is telling me he knows who jacked our spot. "A nigga, named Ghetto. His uncle and 'em went down with the Diablos back in the 90's."

Everybody in the 'A' and their mama had heard about the infamous Diablos.

Shorty Got a Thug

"And you said that to say what?" I question him. "Because I don't give a fuck about that nigga's bloodline. What I wanna know is this, if you already know who the nigga is, why is he still breathing?"

I end the call without allowing him a chance to retort.

*****

They say when it rains, it pours. I believe that shit because bad news keeps coming back to back. First I get a call from Unc's sister telling me that Unc got popped by popo with three bricks.

I handle that.

Two days later Fat Cat is rollin' wit' me; we're following his bitch to a motel out by the airport but Shanteria don't know we're behind her. I've heard from a friend of a friend that Shanteria is creepin' on Fat Cat with the same nigga who flexed him with the counterfeit dough.

We let Shanteria pull into the motel's parking lot and we drive on by. A while later we park where we can observe Shanteria's car. She stays in the motel room for three hours. Finally, she emerges and the nigga does too.

Ca$h

"Is that the same nigga?" I ask Fat Cat.

He nods his head.

It looks like he wanna cry.

I hit Tank up real quick, he's parked across the street. Been sitting there for the past two hours after I called him and told him what was poppin' off.

"Sup, fam," he answers.

"The nigga is about to pull out in a second. He's driving a black Suburban. Take his head off."

"A'ight. I'ma let him get a few miles away from here before I smash him though." I speak into my ear piece.

"That's what's up. One."

Now I'm two cars behind Shanteria. I stay behind her as she hops on I-285. I guess she's headed home, drippy pussy bitch. Fat Cat is quiet. He's wearing a somber look.

"Bruh, the bitch is foul. And you know she knows the nigga flexed on you. The bitch was probably down with the lick. You treat her better than she treats herself and look how she repays you. What if you was at home waiting to eat her pussy? The trifling bitch would let you eat her knowing she just let another nigga run up in it."

I've made my point so I hush.

Not another word is spoken until I pull up to Fat Cat's house. I purposely slow down to allow Shanteria to get inside the house before we drive up.

My nigga and I are parked at the curb in front of his crib. I hand him my Ruger. "Go handle your business." It's an order.

"Nah, fam, don't make me do it," he begs off.

I insist but that only makes Fat Cat beg harder.

"A'ight, I'ma allow you a chance to let her explain. Hit me and let me know the business," I relent with an exasperated sigh.

Fat Cat's smile shows relief. "Thanks, fam," he exhales.

"It's all love bruh. La familia."

We touch fists and Fat Cat lumbers his large frame out of my whip. He's almost to his side door when I run up on him and crush his weak ass. *Bok! Bok! Bok!! Bok! Bok!*

I show him no mercy.

A family is only as strong as its weakest member.

Ca$h

The clap of the Ruger has obviously been heard by Shanteria. I catch a glimpse of her peeking out of the blinds covering the window to the side door. Thinking fast, I bang on the door. "Shanteria! Open the door, this is Brazen. A nigga just rode by and shot Fat Cat. Hurry up!"

She opens the door looking worried.

I smile menacingly and spray all her shit out the back of her head.

Ten minutes away from my latest carnage I hit Tank up. "Did you handle that?" I ask. His answer makes me smile.

CHAPTER 40
<u>Carmen</u>

"Smile, baby. Why you always so uptight?" The nigga has the nerve to ask me.

"I'm not fuckin *uptight!* If you wanna see a bitch uptight keep tryna play me." I threaten him.

I met Desmond at The Underground before I hooked up with Brazen. In the heat of the moment, one night, I allowed Desmond to hit it raw. When I found out that I was pregnant, I had already fucked Brazen too, but that was a month after Desmond. I figured the times were close enough for me to put the baby on Brazen, niggas get tricked like this all the time. There's no telling how many stupid ass niggas are raising kids that they *think* is theirs.

Me, I'm just doing what a bitch has to do. Don't hate the playa, hate the game.

We're in the parking lot of Wal-Mart on Jonesboro Road. I'm in the passenger seat of his BMW,

170

about to show my high yellow ass if he continues patronizing me. "Nigga, I'm eight months pregnant, with your baby, and you wanna act all shitty when I ask your ass for some money? Don't make me show my other side, 'cause it won't be pretty." I rant.

Desmond says, "Carmen, why should I continue to dish out money to you when you've already told me that you're not going to allow me to be a part of the child's life once it's born?"

I look at him like he's special. "Desmond, I've explained this to you fifty times already. You're married with a family already—you don' t want to mess that up. And I'm not no sideline bitch. Brazen thinks this is his child, he knows nothing about you and I plan to keep it that way. When I can, I'll sneak off and let you see the baby."

"That's not good enough," he replies.

"It *has* to be! Trust, you don't wanna go against Brazen."

Desmond is quiet; he's probably considering my warning. He's a square, he does not want the type of

171

beef that might pop off if we disclose our deception to Brazen and neither do I.

Finally Desmond forks over some cash.

Driving away from Wal-Mart, I press *67 to block out my number then I call Brazen. I have to trick him into answering my calls now. Since I no longer make runs for Brazen he has really started acting funky. I'm about fed up with his shit.

Just when I think I'm about to be sent to voicemail, Brazen answers. "Sup?"

"Why do I have to disguise my number for you to accept my got damn call?" I go off before I realize it.

"Bitch don't call my phone talkin' slick. State your business and get off my phone," Brazen snaps back, hurting my feelings.

"I need money for groceries and I have a doctor's appointment in the morning, would you please go with me?"

"I'ma be out of town. I'll send Dee to go with you."

"It's not Dee's fuckin' responsibility. I want *you* to go with me. And I want you to take me grocery shopping. If you don't do it, fuck you!"

"Nah, fuck you! Starve bitch!"

Ca$h

"I wish I could spit through this phone, dead into your no-good ass face!" I shout.

"And get your ass beat to sleep."

His disrespect makes me lose it. I can't control my response. My mouth says, "Nigga, don't forget I witnessed you kill a man in cold blood. Shit on me and I'll send your black ass to prison for the rest of your natural life!"

"What did you just say?" Brazen grits.

I drop the phone and cry. I know that I have just fucked up. I see images in my mind of the man Brazen killed that night for no reason at all. I pick my phone back up and put it to my ear. "Brazen, I'm sorry," I apologize.

He is no longer on the line.

I pull over to the side of the road where I begin to hyper-ventilate.

CHAPTER 41
Brazen

I've called a meeting with my team to discuss the state of our affairs. I also want to explain to them why they are not to attend Fat Cat's funeral. However, right now I gotta go by this stupid trick Carmen's house and calm her the fuck down.

On the drive to Carmen's spot I hit Butta up and give her the game plan on something very important. We discuss how I want the business handled. "I don't want to see him at the meeting. The nigga is hot and I'm not sure we can trust him. *La Familia,* baby girl. That's over everything," I end the conversation.

I knock on Carmen's door. Of course, she's afraid to let me in. A few slick words and I hear the lock being disengaged. I step inside and close the door behind me.

"You think this is a game?"

I step towards Carmen with my banger out. She retreats two steps back.

"I'm sorry, Brazen." Backing away another few steps.

I grab her by the hair and force the banger in her mouth.

"Don't ever threaten me!" I grit.

Carmen is shaking; she's terrified.

I look her in the eye and squeeze the trigger repeatedly.

Click! Click! Click! Click!

I reach in my pocket and pull out the loaded clip. I put it up to her face so that she can see it.

"Next time my gun won't be empty," I promise her right before she faints.

A week later Carmen and I are good. All of my business isn't though.

Silk finally got at Ghetto but he did it recklessly, taking out two innocent bystanders in the process. I'm so heated, me and Silk almost come to blows. If Tank hadn't grabbed me I don't know what would have happened because niggas ain't fighting these days.

Real talk, I'm thinking about deading Silk.

CHAPTER 42
<u>Silk</u>

Up until now, I've been silent. I just sat back and let Brazen drive this car. I play the background but I bow down to no man. Brazen should know that. I'm a 90's baby, another nigga can't tell me shit.

I roll with the team but I'm not on Brazen's dick like Dee and 'em are. Maddafact, I'm just sitting back watching, plotting my takeover. I'ma let Brazen build his shit up then I'ma jack him for everything—his position and his life.

Nigga think he can check me, I ain't his bitch. My gun makes the beef cook just as quickly as his. What Brazen don't understand is I'ma young boss. I was born to give orders, not to follow them. So I'm just biding my time.

I know that the team is loyal to Brazen so when I strike I'ma smash everyone: Brazen, that dyke Dee, and her bitch Butta. Tank and Marquis can get it too. I don't have to smash Unc, he's on his way out anyway.

Ca$h

I'm still sizzling hot over the way Brazen talked to a nigga earlier. Fam tested my G, fa real! He just don't know, Tank saved that ass. I was a second away from reaching for my waist. Had I brought the *nine* out, Brazen would be in the morgue.

It's gucci, his time is coming.

CHAPTER 43

Butta

"What time do you have, Young Boy?" I kid Marquis as I get off of I-20 and head for the Dogwood subdivision, tonight's destination.

"Almost ten o'clock."

"Ok, I told him we'd be there no later than 10:15 P.M. How you feeling?"

"Pumped. I'm ready to crush this nigga. If it's one thing I hate, it's a snitch. Old heads should know better," Marquis bristles.

We pull up to Unc's house; Marquis is so hyped he's trying to get out of the car before it comes to a complete stop. I place a hand on his elbow.

"Patience, Li'l Boy."

"I got your *li'l boy*," he tosses back.

I ignore the innuendo and quickly go over the instructions Brazen gave me.

"So we smashing everybody up in there, right?" asks Marquis, as if I hadn't made it clear enough.

178

Ca$h

"Yep. Brazen said Unc's wife probably knows too much and their son is sixteen, he's old enough to testify so he gets it too."

"I ain't got no problem with it, he's just a victim of bad relations. His pops shouldn't be a snitch." Marquis is stroking his burner as lovingly as one might stroke a Persian cat.

I don't tell Marquis that we don't know for certain that Unc flipped. It doesn't even matter, Brazen wants him dead so it's been written.

Young Boy reads my mind. He says, "You got mad love for Brazen, don't you?"

"Real recognize real—and with me that's not just a cliché." I emphasize.

Marquis replies, "I'm glad you know that because when this is over I wanna chill with you. I know Dee keeps you happy but you gotta want some *real dick* from a *real nigga* once in a while."

"What I might want is none of your business, Juvenile Delinquent. And if I did want some real dick it would be attached to a grown ass man, not a little jail bait nigga."

Shorty Got a Thug

I love clowning Marquis's young sexy ass. But he's unperturbed. He has the shield of arrogant youth on his side.

"Shorty, this shit right here won't get you cased up, but it will get you sprung." He grins and rubs my thigh.

"And the very thing you desire might get you murked. Think about that while you sitting over there probably on bone." I reach over and politely move his hand from where it has no business being.

"I ain't scared." He smiles brashly.

"Probably not, because a *child* knows no better. I'm about to see how gangsta you are. Let's go in here and create a massacre," I say.

We both get out of the car and shut our doors at the same time.

Unc, who's expecting us, let's us in without any suspicion. He thinks we've come to drop off money that Brazen is giving him to pay for the legal representation he'll need to fight the trafficking charge.

By the time Marquis and I leave up out of there, Unc doesn't need anything but some pall bearers. Ditto for his wife and son.

CHAPTER 44
Dee

"Why are you screaming in my fuckin' face?" Butta yells back at me.

"I asked you where the fuck you been!" I repeat. I jack her up and slam her against the bedroom wall. "Answer me bitch or I'm going in your jaw!" My fist is clenched.

"Oh, I'm a bitch now, huh?" She shoots back, tryna reverse the guilt.

"Answer the question: *where the fuck you been for the past three days? Huh, Butta?*"

"Handling that thing for Brazen," she stutters.

"For three days? That's your final answer?" I feel unbridled anger rising in my chest.

"It's the truth," Butter maintains.

I know she's lying, it doesn't take seventy-two hours to murk a muthafucka. My hands go around her throat.

"Get—off—of—me." She gags.

181

Shorty Got a Thug

"You fucked Marquis, didn't you? You sucked his dick and you let him eat your pussy! Bitch, you probably let him fuck you in the ass!"

"You're sick!" she coughs.

"Sick of listening to you lie!" *Whap*! I pop her in the nose, drawing blood.

Butta tries to fight back but in my anger I'm much too strong for her. I sling her ass around like a wet mop. Then I punch her in that lying mouth of hers. She crumples to the floor crying.

"Get up bitch or I'ma kick your teeth out," I snarl and my voice rattles in a loud timbre.

"I told you I didn't fuck him," Butta continues to lie. That just makes me madder.

Whap! I slap spit and blood out of her mouth.

"I don't believe you!" I scream back at her.

In my jealous rage, I forget that it was an abusive relationship with a man that opened the door for me to convince Butta that a girl would treat her better. I beat her like I'm a man myself. She balls up in a knot trying to cover her face and stomach from the fierceness of the kicks I aim at her body while she's on the floor.

182

Ca$h

"I give you my heart and soul and you do me like this? You creep on me? Bitch I'll kill you!" Butta's betrayal has turned me into a monster.

As she lay whimpering on the floor, I feel no remorse. I'm too hurt to feel anything but pain and rage. All along I knew this was Butta's first relationship with a woman. In the beginning I braced myself for the possibility that she might still desire the touch of a man. But now I'm caught up and I have zero understanding.

I look down at her and sneer, "Take your pants off!"

"For what?" she groans.

"So I can smell your pussy to see if you've been fuckin'!"

"Oh, please!" She blows me off.

Now I'm determined to find out. I yank at the tight capri pants she's wearing. Butta kicks at me.

A'ight, I'm through playing with her. I go to my dresser and get my big ass Desert Eagle. I aim it at Butta. "Take those muthafuckas off, right now bitch!" I command.

She knows not to call my bluff. Slowly she wiggles out of her pants and I stick my nose in-between her thighs.

183

Shorty Got a Thug

Inhaling her scent, I grumble, "Your pussy smells like cheap ass hotel soap. Bitch, you fucked him!"

I put the Desert Eagle down and punch the shit out of her. I beat Butta until I'm out of breath.

Later, Butta's face is swollen. I look at her and feel bad. Tears pour out of my eyes, staining my cheeks. It feels like someone has plunged a knife in my heart. Me and Butta were supposed to be the hood version of *Thelma & Louise*. Doesn't she know that I would die for her? I wonder, as I slowly pack my bags.

I already miss Butta, though I haven't even left yet. I plop down on the side of the bed, crying into my hands. "This shit hurts so bad," I sob. "Shorty, why you hurt a bitch like this?"

I try to say more but I can't talk, I'm hurting too bad.

Butta wraps her arms around me. She holds me, saying nothing until my sobs grow faint. Then she says, "I told you I didn't fuck nobody."

I beg of her, "Please don't lie to me. A lie hurts much more than the truth does. Be honest and allow me to deal with it."

Ca$h

"I didn't fuck Marquis. After we dealt with Unc and his family I felt real bad. That woman—Unc's wife—pleaded with us not to kill her son. She never once asked us to spare *her* life. For some strange reason that got to me. I just needed a few days to myself," explains Butta.

I look into her eyes and she's crying too.

The bitch is lying.

CHAPTER 45

<u>Brazen</u>

"Damn, shorty, what the fuck happened to you? Did you run into a brick wall?" I ask Butta. Shorty's face is jacked up.

We're seated on the couch of her living room. Twenty keys, that I just brought her, are on the floor at our feet.

"Dee jumped on me," she confides.

"For what?" I pry.

"Over some bullshit," is all that I can get out of Butta.

Later in the day when I get with Dee on some other *family* business, I ask her what happened with her and Butta.

"She violated," Dee says in a clipped response.

I shake her response off, it explains nothing. I need to know what happened to make Dee fuck Butta up so bad. I press Dee into telling me what popped off. I listen quietly

186

while she shares her suspicions. She ends by saying, "Butta wouldn't be shook up about murking a teenager or about any of Unc's wife's pleas. She can tell that lie to someone else."

I consider her point without commenting on it. I don't know what to believe. What Dee said makes sense on one hand, but on the other hand why would Butta and Marquis violate a member of the team like that?

"Let me talk to both of them. I'ma get some straight answers," I say, reserving judgment until I speak with Marquis and Butta.

"They'll both lie," Dee predicts.

I tell her that I pity 'em if they do.

Whoever was the first to say, *more money, more problems* had to be a boss. Shit was a lot simpler when I was a block hugger, pitchin' stones. Now that I'm touching major work there's always some other shit in the game. The outside shit is to be expected, it's the *in-the-family* shit that has me stressed.

I scoop up Marquis.

As soon as he's in the truck I drive off. I head away from the Bluff, which is where I scooped him up from. Hitting I-20 West, driving aimlessly, I turn down the music in the truck so that we can hear one another. "Marquis," I start, "loyalty to the family is a must. Do you understand me?"

"Yeah, I understand you, fam." He nods.

"We don't cross one another. We don't steal from each other, we don't lie to one another, and we never ever flip. You hear what I'm saying?"

"I hear you."

"Ok, youngin, let me go straight for the jugular. Dee feels like you're fuckin' Butta. If you are, I can understand it. I mean, Butta is a bad bitch. The average nigga can't turn her down. Are you hearing me?"

"Yes sir."

"Youngin, if you fucked Butta tell me now. Just keep it *one hunnid* and we'll go straighten it with Dee, because she's feeling some kinda way. Now before you respond let's make it clear that I know it takes two to tango. Butta violated too, if y'all took it there. See, fuckin' Dee's chick is just like stealing from her."

"I didn't do it. Fam, I already told Dee that. Shorty calling me up talking about what she'll do to me like I'm some lame. I know Dee get it in, but I ain't no slouch," says Marquis, getting it off his chest.

Ca$h

I shake my head in exasperation. This is the type of shit that divides a strong team. "Youngin, swear to me that it never happened."

"It never happened, big homie." Marquis gives me his word.

"Don't let me find out otherwise," I warn.

These are my last words to him on the subject.

A few hours later I'm giving the same speech to Butta that I gave to Marquis. When I conclude I ask her, "Tell me the truth, Butta. Did you fuck him? Please don't lie to me."

Butta looks me in the eye and responds. I accept her answer as the truth.

*****

For two days I sit alone in the five bedroom house I leased out in Dunwoody. I answer no calls except those from my connect informing me that he'll have a shipment brought to me soon. It's a big relief not to have to send anyone to M-I-YAYO to pick up the work. Those days are months in the rear.

Shorty Got a Thug

I look out the large picture window in my living room and for the first time in my life I get nostalgic. Perhaps it's because my twenty-eighth birthday is only a few weeks away.

Outside the leaves have disappeared from the trees. Winter has forced its will on the city much like my clique has done to the game. The peace of mind I get resting my head out here in the suburbs is in stark contrast to the chaos of the inner city where I've helped drive the body count higher than ever.

I have it all at my finger tips: money and power. But I no longer have the person who was most important to me. Ni is gone and I can't find her. Her house is vacant and there's a FOR RENT sign in the front yard. She is no longer employed at Atlanta Medical Center. When I call her cell phone it's not in service and Ni's mother claims to not know where Ni has disappeared to.

Real talk, I'm fucked up in the head. They say you never miss your water until your well runs dry. I can attest to that now. What good is it for me to have riches if I don't have Ni? I can't enjoy the coffee without my Dark Cream.

Cash

Other females can't replace her. In fact, I don't even get down like that no more.

Missing Ni has me in a melancholy mood. I do my best to put on my game face as I arrive at the usual spot where team meetings are held. I walk into the basement feeling the weight of the game on my shoulders. Without uttering formalities I take my seat at the head of the table. Silk, Dee, Tank and Butta are already seated.

"Where's Marquis?" Dee asks Butta. I can't tell if she's being sarcastic or not.

I announce, "We'll proceed without him." I fold my hands on top of the table and look at the top management of my team. *How much loyalty do we have to one another?* That's the question that is foremost on my mind.

Looking past my four comrades I see the many boxes filled with kilos stacked against the walls. One hundred bricks of fish scale that my connect delivered to me earlier today. That work has become my personal god. Our god.

Amongst the stacked boxes there is a lone bowling bag. Inside that bowling bag is something that represents what a true family is supposed to be about: loyalty. I clear my throat and address my fam.

"More money, more problems," I begin with a drawn out sigh. "When we began this journey we were as one. We were supposed to be about family first. *La Familia.* So what's happening to us? Is it the money? Is it the power? Jealousy or envy?"

I look from one person to the next. My voice is low and even, but strong.

"A house divided will fall." I stand up and walk around the table to the empty chair that Fat Cat used to occupy. I remind the crew that Fat Cat was weak. "So he had to be put down." I topple over the empty chair.

I take a few steps before stopping at a second unoccupied chair. "Unc was suspect after he got popped with that work. He started moving shaky. I couldn't trust him with the family's secrets so I had to put him down. Sometimes you have to cut off the finger to save the hand."

I kick over Unc's empty chair. Then I slowly walk over to where the bowling bag is hidden behind the stacked boxes. I pick up the bowling bag and bring it back to table with me.

192

Ca$h

Stopping where Butta is seated I say, "Loyalty is everything. Never forget it!" I sit the bowling bag on the floor between my feet and retrieve ten champagne glasses from a box that is underneath the table. I carefully arrange the glasses in the center of the table. All eyes look on, puzzled. Soon I will blow their minds.

I reach down between my legs and pick up the bowling bag, setting it down on the table and zipping it open. I reach inside and bring out a human head. I stick a finger in each eye socket and my thumb in the mouth, holding the head like a bowling ball.

The dismembered human head leaks blood from the severed neck when I roll it towards the champagne glasses, throwing a perfect strike. The head comes to a stop at the edge of the table furthest away from me. I walk down to that end and look down at the dismembered head. Marquis's lifeless eyes stare up, seeing nothing.

I look up and stare into the faces of my team, one member at a time. Each of them wear a look of shock. I fix my intense gaze on Butta and hold it there.

"I warned him not to lie to me. I'm glad you told me the truth, Butta, because for you that wouldn't have been a pretty look. I point at Marquis's head for emphasis as everyone backs up a bit from the gory mess before them. I go back to the head of the table and take a seat on my throne with my hands folded in front of me on the table.

Four mouths are open when I take in my teams' reaction. For effect I continue on with family business as if the head on the table isn't even there. Thirty minutes later, business concludes. In closing, I direct Butta to apologize to Dee for wronging her. "And make sure you take care of that," I further direct her, indicating the head.

Butta tearfully apologizes to her lover. I watch them hug and I know that from this point on there will be no more problems between them.

Leaving the stash house I receive a text message telling me that Carmen is in labor. *If it ain't one thing it's another.*

CHAPTER 46
Dee

Butta' s entire body shakes with ecstasy as my tongue dances back and forth across her clitoris. I hold open her wet folds and suck inside gently. Tears trickle down my face, they mix together with Butta's honey juice.

I sniffle back more tears as I continue to stimulate Butta's love button while internally wrestling with the heartbreak that she has caused me.

"Umm! I'm about to cummmm!" she moans softly.

The evidence of Butta's satisfaction tastes better than candy. I smack my lips then slide up her body so that we are now clit to clit in a wet, squishy, hot tangle. "Oh yessss, umm, let me lick my sweetness off of your mouth," whispers Butta.

She sucks my bottom lip and arches her steamy pussy up against mine. My own pussy is soaking the satin sheets beneath us. I've never been so sopping wet before.

195

Shorty Got a Thug

Butta's Brazilian waxed pussy is causing an inferno in mine. It feels so good yet I'm hurting so bad. Without warning, I get up and sit on the side of the bed. My head is down in my hands.

"What's wrong, baby?" asks Butta, sitting up.

"I keep seeing him make love to you, entering you in a way that I can never do. Tell me the truth, did he make you come?"

Butta doesn't answer so I know that means yes. I bawl like a baby. I feel her gently take me into her arms and kiss me. "Baby, I know that I hurt you, but please try to forgive me. I'll never betray you again. I thought that I was missing something. I needed to do that, now I know that I don't need it. I love you, Dee. I promise you that no one else will ever touch me gain."

Now Butta's tears mix with mine.

"I love you so much," I whisper to her. Then we just hold each other.

CHAPTER 47

Brazen

By the time I make it to the hospital Carmen has already given birth to a baby boy. When I hold the baby, I feel no connection at all. Maybe I'm heartless.

I study the baby's every feature; I see none that resemble any of mine. I refuse to sign the birth certificate until we've taken a paternity test.

Carmen goes off!

"Miss me with the theatrics," I snap. "If the paternity test proves that I'm the father, we're good. Until then I'm not signing shit."

The following day I'm on a flight to Miami to fuck with my connect. This trip ain't about business, I'm going to look at a house out Biscayne that I might want to buy. Whenever I get out of the game, I'ma find Ni and we're gonna move to Florida and make a bunch of children.

In Miami I end up falling in love with this stucco-styled five bedroom home on Miami Beach. "That's the one." I tell the realtor.

Shorty Got a Thug

I wish my baby was with me to see it," I say to myself. Ni is still heavy on my mind.

I hit a few night clubs, rolling with my connect's younger brother. Bitches jock my swag but I turn down all offers. I guess I'm on some real grown man shit these days.

Two days later when I touch back down in the 'A', all hell has broken loose.

Residents of a Southwest Atlanta neighborhood where we have several trap houses held an all-night prayer vigil to drive drugs out of the community, I'm told by Dee. "Silk felt some kinda way about it so he commanded us to do a drive-by. I told that stupid nigga that a drive-by was a ridiculous and reckless idea," recounts Dee.

"And I backed her because that was some real hot boy shit. The holy rollers weren't stopping anything. They would've gotten a little face time on the news then the hood would continue doing what it do. But Silk wouldn't listen, he gathered up some of our young street soldiers and those fools shot up the prayer tents. Two old ladies got killed and a little girl is barely clinging to her life," pipes in Butta.

Ca$h

I frown at the foolishness of the assault. It served no purpose other than to stroke Silk's ego. I glare at Tank who, so far, has said nothing.

"What about you Tank? What did you have to say about it?" I ask.

His eyes raise up to meet mine. Tank, who is a dude of few words, makes no excuses, he says honestly, "I didn't have an opinion, I just followed the orders of the one you left in charge. I'm a soldier, that's what soldiers do."

I can't do nothing but respect what Tank just said.

I whip out my cell phone and punch in Silk's number. Rick Ross's *BMF* plays while I wait for Silk to answer. Thirty seconds into the song, Silk finally answers. "Fam, what's poppin?" His voice is jovial as if it's all good in the hood.

"What's poppin'? Nigga, some heads about to get popped around this bitch!" I spazz out. I really wish I could go through the phone and crush that ass.

"Who you talking to?" His response and his tone is a direct challenge to my power. I saw this coming.

"Tell me where you're at, nigga, and I'll come answer you to your face."

199

Shorty Got a Thug

"I'm over in Hightower. Come holler at me, I'm not going nowhere."

I end the call without replying. If this is what he wants, I'ma give it to him. I storm out of the stash house, hop in my truck and zoom off, tires screeching.

I'm doing a hunnid miles per hour, anxious to get to that ass. I reach the apartments where I know Silk is at in record time. I whip up dead in the middle of him congregating with a crowd of niggas, none of whom I'm familiar with. It's winter time so I'm rocking a thick jacket with a fur-lined hood. Hopping out of my truck, I reach inside my jacket and grab my Ruger.

Butta, Dee, and Tank whip up behind me in two separate vehicles. Several of the dudes that Silk is talking to recognize me. They part to let me through their circle. Silk is sitting on the hood of his black 600 series Benz. I step right up in his space.

"You want some of me?" I grit.

He coolly pulls on the blunt that he's smoking.

"You can't talk all breezy to me and expect not to get it back the same way, homie. Nigga, we put our pants on the same way." He coughs from the loud he's smoking.

Ca$h

"I can talk anyway I wanna when you fuck up what I put together!" I check him. "Now if you gotta problem with something I said, let's make the news." My black steel toolie is locked and loaded.

I notice that Silk has a banger in his hand that's down by his side. The darkness of the night had concealed it until now. If he so much as flinches I'ma open up his breast plate.

"It's whateva with me, bruh," says Silk. His banger is aimed at my stomach.

Dee says, "*La familia*!"

Butta echoes her.

Me and Silk stare each other down. Neither one of us bat an eye. Finally Silk lowers his banger, letting it rest on the hood of his whip. But he's still gripping it. I lower the Ruger to my side. I look at the niggas crowded around hoping to see some gun play.

"This is *family* business, y'all let us have this li'l bit," I say to the crowd.

Dee and 'em whip them thangs out, silently commanding the crowd to push on. Still they don't move far away until Silk yells to them, "I'm good. Y'all can fall back."

Shorty Got a Thug

I peep the move, he's built up his own team. The line has been drawn in the sand so there's no need to say anything. I walk back to my truck. My three loyal comrades follow my lead.

"What's understood doesn't have to be said," I comment to them before we get into our whips and drive off.

CHAPTER 48

Narration

Brazen immediately cleared out the stash house. He switched up all of his moves in anticipation of any way that Silk might try to come at him. They were enemies now, Brazen could not afford to sleep on his ex-lieutenant. Silk's mind was too treacherous to be taken lightly.

Brazen could feel it in his soul, the time to walk away from the game was nearing. However, he wanted to walk away on his own accord. His gangsta was much too official to allow himself to be forced out. And when he did let his gun cool off, he didn't want to leave alive a single enemy that might rise up and come for his head.

All enemies didn't pack a banger. One in particular held weapons just as lethal as the Ruger that Brazen held down by his side as he slid the door key into the lock and heard it click.

With a gloved hand Brazen turned the door knob and crept inside, hurrying to close the door to keep out the cold gust of wind that whooshed at his back. There was a brief bitter cold on the back of Brazen's neck; it was nothing compared to the coldness in his heart.

The apartment was quiet and dark.

The thick carpet silenced Brazen's footsteps as he crept towards the bedroom. He stopped outside the bedroom door to put the homemade silencer on the Ruger.

The bedroom door stood wide open. Peeking around the door frame he saw that the person that he had come to kill was in bed asleep. He smiled derisively as he eyed the frame under the blanket. *Slick ass bitch*!

The paternity results were back, and in the famous words of Maury, the results had told Brazen: you—are—not—the—father.

Seeing those results earlier in the week had been a big relief. Now Brazen didn't have to be torn over what he was about to do. Like a silent assassin he moved quietly towards the canopy style bed. He came to a sudden stop a step away and stood in his place. Brazen was shocked!

There were two figures in bed, Carmen and some nigga. *Grimey 'til the end* thought Brazen. It didn't matter though. He cared nothing about who Carmen fucked. Brazen's only concern was the secrets of his that Carmen held.

He walked quietly around the other side of the bed. The nigga in bed with Carmen stirred just as Brazen placed the Ruger against his temple.

Boc! Boc!

The sound was muffled but the results weren't changed by the silencer attached to the Ruger. Dude's brain matter showered out onto the sheet beneath his head, some sprayed in Carmen's face. She blinked open her eyes and was staring at a sealed fate.

"Brazen!" she gasped, shooting up, placing her back against the headboard, and a hand over her heart. Even in the scant lighting in the room her eyes bulged and showed fear.

Brazen put a finger to his mouth.

"Shhhh!"

"Oh my god!" She was terrified by the murderous look in Brazen's eyes.

Carmen looked over at Desmond whose head was outlined in a puddle of blood. She opened her mouth to scream but the sound was cut off by the Ruger.

Boc! Boc! Now there was no chance that she could ever be heard.

Shorty Got a Thug

"Run tell that!"

On the way out of the room Brazen stopped and peered inside the bassinette that was against the wall. Seeing that the baby had kicked his blanket off of him, Brazen covered the baby then disappeared into the night.

CHAPTER 49

Brazen was not the only night stalker. Only time would prove whether or not he was the most vicious.

Silk was friends with the night himself and he was on a mission. Dressed in all black he sat inside the used Durango that he had recently bought for the purpose of being able to move incognito. A few weeks ago he had taken a half dozen members of his new squad with him to hit Brazen's stash house. The lick had netted them nothing, the stash house had been empty. Brazen had been one step ahead.

Tonight Silk shrugged off the previous misfortune, this time he would not move in vain.

From where he was parked he could see the house clearly. He sat in silence, exhibiting the true patience of a predator, waiting to pounce on its prey. When the opportunity arose Silk leaped out of the Durango. He was breathing on the back of Tank's neck just as Tank let himself into his own house.

With the banger to the back of Tank's head, Silk reached around Tank's wide body and removed Tank's fo-fo from his waist. In less than a minute Silk had Tank in plastic cuffs.

Tank sat on the floor bleeding from several gashes in his head.

"C'mon, homie, don't make me pistol whip you again. Call your boy and convince him to come out here," huffed Silk. He had damn near ran out of breath cracking Tank's hard ass head.

"You might as well kill me and save yourself some time. You know how I rock, *La* familia to the grave," replied Tank, stoically.

"Nigga, Brazen must be fucking you cause you way more loyal to him than he would be to you. Was he loyal to Fat Cat? What about Marquis? Was it *La familia* with Brazen when he murked youngin over a piece of pussy that wasn't even his?"

"Youngin violated then he lied," replied Tank who wasn't so much as *wincing* from the sharp bolts of pain that shot through his head where he had been clumped by Silk with the fo-fo.

"Did Fat Cat lie?" sneered Silk.

"Fat Cat was weak."

Ca$h

"Was Unc weak or a liar? And don't try to tell me that Unc was about to flip. I'm not even tryna hear that shit. Unc was doing this shit longer than any of us, he wasn't scared to do a bid. Brazen slumped Unc for nothing," reasoned Silk, who was pacing the living room back and forth.

Tank started to try to explain that Brazen crushed Unc to protect the family, but he knew that his words would change nothing. Tank's fate was already sealed, Silk was just toying with him.

Silk stood over Tank. He looked down at the bleeding man and offered him back his life. "I tell you what, homie. I ain't got no beef with you; me and you have always been good. Give me Brazen. Call him up and convince him that you need to see him ASAP. When he shows up we'll smash him together. Then we can team up, you and me."

"Nah, bruh. Bury me a G," Tank said with honor for the code of the streets.

"That's how you want it?"

"Give it to me the way I lived it," replied Tank. He stared death in the face without buckling his knees.

Shorty Got a Thug

Death stared right back at him, in the form of Silk's fo-fo. It roared loud and angry and the stare down was over, just that quick.

Silk walked into the bedroom of his condo. He tossed a book bag full of money on the dresser. It was the cheddar that he had found at Tank's house after smashing him. Silk's girl, Fatima, stirred out of her sleep at the clunking sound that the heavy book bag made when it landed on the mahogany dresser. She sat up in bed, shook a strand of golden braids out of her face, then wiped sleep from her eyes.

"What time is it?" Her usually sweet voice sounded scratchy.

"Two in the morning," answered Silk.

"Ugh! I have an early class in the morning," groaned Fatima. She was in her sophomore year at Georgia State University.

"Go back to sleep, baby girl." The gentle way that Silk spoke to Fatima was a contradiction to the beast he was in the streets.

Fatima had been his boo for almost a year now. Silk kept her far away from the dirt that he did. She

210

didn't know any of his friends and more importantly none of Silk's enemies knew Fatima, nor where he and she rested at.

Or so Silk thought.

Brazen, like always, was one step ahead.

CHAPTER 50

"Dee, have you or Butta heard from Tank?" asked Brazen.

"I haven't heard from him in a couple days," recalled Dee. "Let me check with Butta, hold on."

Brazen waited nervously for Dee to return to the phone. He was praying that she would come back with some good news, although he had a strong premonition that something had happened to Tank. It was unlike Tank to go days without hollerin'.

"Butta says she hasn't heard from him either," reported Dee.

They found Tank on the living room floor of his house. He had been dogged out. Butta wept in Dee's arms. Brazen wept silently inside. Tank had been the last of a dying breed. Brazen knew that, though he had no way of knowing just how gallant Tank had been in the minutes before he got slumped.

"Silk did this," guessed Brazen correctly, "Let's bury our comrade then we'll deal with that snake ass

212

muthafucka. His words came out heavy with pain. The family, which at one time was eight members, was now down to but three.

Brazen spared no expense laying Tank to rest. He, Butta and Dee sat side by side at the funeral service, in the back row of the church's pew. Butta wept throughout the service. Dee shed a few silent tears. So did Brazen, but his tears were concealed behind dark shades.

After the three of them said their final goodbyes to their fallen homie, they went back to Brazen's house to reminisce about Tank and to plan strategy. It was dark outside when Butta and Dee bounced. Brazen was at home, alone with his thoughts.

Sitting in his black leather recliner, in what he called his music room, Brazen laid back and listened to Biggie rap about beef. The slain rap star's lyrics seemed to speak about what Brazen was presently dealing with.

Brazen reclined further back and drifted off to sleep. He awoke an hour later with a clear mind. He knew that his short reign was over. Not because he had been knocked off of his throne. It was simply that he was no longer hungry.

I'm going out with a bang! he decided.

213

The next day Brazen went to see Mrs. Smiley, Niesha's mother.

Mrs. Smiley stood in the doorway as if she had no intentions at all of inviting Brazen in. Brazen overlooked her stiffness; he knew that he had earned her ire. "Hi, Ma," he spoke affectionately, placing a kiss on her cheek.

"Don't you 'Ma' me," she scolded him for old and new.

"Yeah, I know Ma, I been a real bad boy. But I promise you that I'm ready to change."

"Phoey!" snipped Mrs. Smiley, stepping aside to let him in nevertheless.

She shut the door closing out the cold whistle of winter. She led Brazen into her den where they sat and talked in front of a wood burning fireplace. Brazen apologized, sincerely, for all that he had put her daughter through.

Niesha's mom listened, wanting to believe Brazen, because she knew how much Niesha loved and missed him. "It's almost over, Ma," he promised. "I have some things to wrap up. Those things may cost me my life. So I want to leave something with you to give to Ni if I don't live to see her again."

Mrs. Smiley studied Brazen's face to see if he was serious. She saw that indeed he was, but she didn't dare ask for details. Her final response was a warning to Brazen to be careful.

Brazen promised her that he would.

He made several trips out to his truck. On the last trip he returned carrying a safe. Brazen sat the safe down in the middle of the floor then stood up with a groan. Next to the safe were three duffel bags.

"I'm almost afraid to ask what's inside," admitted Niesha's mother.

"It's nothing but money," revealed Brazen. Anticipating her protest, he quickly added, "No one knows I brought it here. Everything that I hustled for, in the streets, is inside those bags and that safe. I have gunshot wounds on my body. I've been back and forth to prison. I've lost good friends who are now dead and gone. I've lost Ni, most of all. I'm not saying it was worth it, but that's the road that I chose. All I'm asking you to do is to hold on to that money. If I don't come back for it in a couple of weeks, you know what happened. And in that case, I want Ni to have everything. Because my choices were for her, too."

215

Shorty Got a Thug

Mrs. Smiley asked, "What makes you so sure that I know how to contact my daughter?" Her coyness earned a flash of a smile from Brazen.

"Ma, do I have to answer that?"

"No, but there is one question that I need answered, and I want an honest answer from you. Will you promise to give me that?"

"Yes, Ma. What is it you need to know?"

Mrs. Smiley looked Brazen in the eye and asked him if he had anything to do with Carmen's death.

"Anything at all?" she reemphasized.

Brazen, being street savvy, and having endured countless interrogations from police, held a mean poker face. He inflected a look that displayed part shock and part hurt that she would even consider such a thing possible.

"Absolutely not, "he replied, straight-faced.

A look of relief washed over Mrs. Smiley. She apologized for asking the question. Then she stood up and gave him a motherly hug.

Before Brazen left, she told him something that made him smile. Something that gave him every reason in the world to be the last man standing when the bullets stopped flying.

CHAPTER 51

Brazen got with Dee and Butta to check on the progress of the latest mission he had given them. "It's going down tomorrow night," Butta informed him. "I'ma hit you up once I get them niggas cuffed up."

"How do you plan to handle them both? Don't you need some help?" Brazen worried.

"Nope. Trust, I'ma have Andre and Boony so at ease, they won't know what hit them until they hear the click clack. Both of them like to pop pills and snort powder. I have them thinking that we're gonna get fucked up and freaked all night." Butta grinned. She was pleased at her own cleverness.

Brazen worried that the pills might not knock the niggas out. "You wanna try one?" offered Butta.

"Hell no."

"If they don't work I guess a bitch is gonna be in a situation." She hunched her shoulders as if to say it was no big thing.

"Let me find out," enjoined Dee.

Shorty Got a Thug

Butta playfully rolled her eyes and gave Dee the finger.

Dee responded by picking a pillow up off the sofa and tossing it at her. Brazen who was sitting between the two ignored their playfulness, deep down he understood love.

"Don't worry, Dee, I'ma be close by. Trust, I'm not gon' let them niggas touch shorty. I've been waiting to serve those two youngins ever since they wet me up. What I did to their Uncle Juvie ain't gonna seem like shit compared to what I'ma do to them," promised Brazen.

He was leaving no loose ends when he stepped away from the game.

"What about the twenty blocks we had left, y'all got rid of 'em yet?" He looked at Dee.

She reported, "We have eight left. I'm driving those down to Savannah tomorrow evening. I have a cousin there who wants all eight."

"Is your cousin on the up and up?"

"Yeah, he's official. You don't even have to worry about my end. Just promise me you'll make sure my boo is safe and sound while I'm gone," she asked of him.

"Shorty, I got this," said Brazen.

Ca$h

Meanwhile, in another part of the 'A', Silk was getting it in. His new connect had hit him off with thirty bricks. Seated at the head of a small conference table, in the back room of a store front building that he had rented, Silk was joined by six members of his new clique which was being called M&M, money and murder.

The six youths seated around Silk at the table had been chosen by him to be his lieutenants. Each of them had recently helped Silk wipe out all competition up and down Bankhead Highway. Police were still busy unstacking the bodies and identifying the slain.

Silk stood, looking around the table from face to face. He was nearing the conclusion of the speech that he was giving. "... so if any one of you doubt my ability to lead this family," he said as he walked around the table and placed a fo-fo in the hand of one of his mans. "...put a bullet in my head now."

He had stolen Brazen's gangsta.

CHAPTER 52

Butta clamped the handcuffs around Boony's wrist then smiled down at her handiwork. Boony was knocked the fuck out. So was his cousin Andre, who was on the bed next to Boony.

The pills had done what Butta was told they would do. She was thankful for that because she hadn't been looking forward to plan B.

Butta eased out of the motel room and knocked on the door next to it. "Yeah?" answered Brazen.

"It's me. It's your show now."

Recognizing Butta's voice, Brazen slid out of the room. "Let's wipe the room down then you can go on home, I'll handle it from there."

"Are you sure?" Butta asked.

Brazen gave her his assurance by nodding his head.

Back in the room where Boony and Andre were knocked out, Brazen wearing gloves removed the cuffs off of their wrists after duct-taping them. Butta's prints might be left on the steel cuffs.

Ca$h

Together Brazen and Butta wiped down the room, removed the cover and sheets off of the bed, just on the chance that they contained particles of Butta's hair. "Take these with you when you leave," Brazen pointed to the pile of bedding.

After Butta left, Brazen taped the cousins' feet and gagged their mouths. Then he patiently waited for them to come out from under the effect of the pills. He wanted them to see their mistake; leaving him alive!

Butta spoke into her earpiece as she drove home.

"Everything went as planned. *You know who* is dealing with them now, I'm on my way to the house. Hurry home, bitch, I miss you."

"I miss you more, baby. I'll be home sometime tomorrow night. I want you to have dinner ready, candles burning, wine chilled—and have that kitty cat ready to purr," said Dee, getting her mack on.

Butta blushed.

"You know I will. I'll have the hot oil out and that new thingy that vibrates on both of our clits at the same time. Whew! I'm getting excited just talking about that thing—it's a beast!"

221

"Let me find out," Dee teased.

They continued talking sex until somehow the subject changed to something else. Butta said, "I'll be glad when all of this is over and we can just be in love, happily ever after."

"Yeah, I know, right?" replied Dee. She wanted the same. "But we gotta get Silk first. What he did to Tank was fucked up. Brazen will never walk away until we crush Silk's crusty ass."

"That's true," agreed Butta. "Have you thought about where we'll go after this is over? Brazen says he's moving to Miami Beach, he's already purchased a house down there."

"I wouldn't mind being Brazen's neighbor." *Hint. Hint.*

"Hint, hint my ass! Nope. Not. Nada. I love Brazen but if we move to Florida in close proximity to him, before long he'll have us building up another team. I'm not doing it," protested Butta.

Dee couldn't help but laugh, she could see Brazen doing just that. Brazen was true and true, a thug and a hustla. He was poppin' his gums about retiring

222

from the game, finding Niesha and settling down but Dee couldn't see him doing that for long.

"Dee, I'm not playing. When this is over, it's over. I want to adopt a child and live far away from here. Florida ain't far enough," said Butta.

"Okay boo. Choose a state you want to move to, any place that's not cold. On second thought, it don't matter. It could be the North Pole as long as we're together."

"Aww, that's so sweet. I love you so much," cooed Butta, feeling her emotions stirring.

"I love you more," Dee said once again. Her phone beeped. She saw it was a business call. "Bae, I'ma have to hit you later," she said.

"Okay. Smooches."

"Muah."

Butter removed her earpiece and turned up the volume on the stereo in her car. Monica's singing kept her company until she arrived home. She pulled into her garage, which was connected to her house. Through the garage she entered into her kitchen. The light was off in the kitchen, she had asked Dee to stop turning out all of the lights when she left, Butta hated coming home to a dark house.

Shorty Got a Thug

Running her hand down the nearby wall, Butta clicked the light switch. The kitchen flooded with florescent light. Butta gasped. Silk was seated with both feet propped up on the round glass table. He wore a smirk on his face. What he held in his hand made Butta lose control of her bladder.

"Welcome home, baby girl," Silk taunted, sliding his finger along the cutting edge of a machete. The light bounced off the machete's sharp edge.

Butta swallowed hard. She tried to ease her hand inside the Fendi bag that she was carrying but her arms were quickly pinned to her sides by one of the two goons that had been hiding on either side of the door.

The goons marched Butta over to Silk.

"Butta," Silk said, "I want you to call Brazen and get him over here. I'm not here to play games with you. Each time you refuse to make the call, I'm gonna cut off a finger."

Butta's whole body began to shake. This was one of her worst fears. She had lived by the gun, wasn't it supposed to be that she would die by the same? A quick death that she hadn't saw coming?

Ca$h

Torture by knife was frightening. *It's going to be painful,* feared Butta. Her legs were trembling so bad she could barely keep them underneath her.

Silk ran the sharp tip of the machete down the front of Butta's blouse. With ease, he sliced off a button.

"What you gonna do?" he asked her.

"I'll make the call," she quickly acquiesced.

CHAPTER 53

Andre was the first to come out from under the drug-induced sleep that he had been in for forty minutes. It took Boony a little longer to wake up from the knockout drug, probably because he was much smaller than Andre. At any rate, they were both awake now and aware that they had been suckered into a fucked-up situation.

Brazen looked down on the floor at the bound and gagged youngins. *"What had happened was..."* He said sadistically. Then he laughed.

Apparently Brazen was the only one in the room who found his words funny. There was not a single hint of laughter in either of his captives' eyes.

"Okay, nobody's in a joking mood, I see. So let me get straight down to the business at hand." He raised the Ruger and popped Boony in the head twice. The boy toppled over onto his side. Blood oozed onto Andre's leg.

"Youngin, so you don't die without absolutely knowing; yeah, I killed Juvie. I stood over him and crushed him like I'm about to do you. I respect ya'll gangsta for coming at me. That's loyalty. But when you get at a killa, you can't ever leave him alive. That night at the gas station, you should've shot me in the head. Like this."

Boc! Boc!

Brazen blew Andre's brains out.

Two additional shots in each boy's head made certain that they both would be starring on the obituary page of *The Atlanta Journal and Constitution*. The shots barely made a popping sound.

Brazen unscrewed the noise muzzler from the end of the Ruger and headed out the door. *I told Butta I would be by there once I handled this*, he recalled.

Brazen's plan was to keep her company while Dee was away. With Silk out there somewhere lurking, Brazen didn't want Butta to be alone. Shorty was a *G* with her shit but Silk was sick with his.

Brazen hopped on the interstate. He popped in Biggie's *Life after Death* as he headed to his destination. A light flashed on the passenger seat. Out of his peripheral vision, Brazen noticed it. He reached over, grabbed his cell phone, and answered the call.

"Brazen, this is Butta. *Don't come here they're waiting to kill you! Silk and...*"

He heard the phone being snatched away from Butta, cutting off her frantic cry. Then he heard the most awful scream.

Brazen kept calling Butta's phone back until someone answered. Finally after being sent to voicemail more than a dozen times, a voice Brazen knew all too well answered Butta's phone and began laughing.

"Nigga, if you hurt her, I won't rest until I crush your muthafuckin' ass—that's on all I love!" Brazen declared.

Silk chuckled harder and Brazen could imagine the snide look on his face. "Bruh," replied Silk, "remember what you did to Marquis?" He didn't wait for Brazen to answer. "Well I just did the same thing to Butta and I sat it on top of the bitch's mantel like a trophy," he bragged.

Ca$h

"You just sealed your own death, bitch ass nigga! I'm on my way over there; if you're so gangsta be there when I pull up."

"Nah, pimp, I'll catch you in traffic. You wanna talk to Butta? Oh, my bad, Butta ain't got no head." Silk's maniacal laugh drummed in Brazen's head as Brazen sped towards Butta's house.

Twenty minutes later, Brazen's truck came to a screeching stop in front of Butta's house. Brazen hopped out and ran up in the crib, banger out, ready to die. There was so much blood on the kitchen floor Brazen almost slipped and fell. Butta's headless body was sprawled out in the middle of the floor. Brazen didn't go check the mantel, he did not want to remember baby girl like that. "Shorty, I'm sorry," he said to her beheaded corpse.

Miles away from the ghastly scene Brazen stopped at a pay phone and dialed 911. He gave the operator Butta's address. He did not want Dee to come home tomorrow and walk into a nightmare.

CHAPTER 54

Dee didn't shed a single tear throughout the funeral.
She sat in the front row of the pew along with Butta's
relatives—who at any other time could not stand the
sight of each other—staring straight ahead. Her eyes
were blank. Soulless.

Brazen sat directly behind her, but they
approached the stage together to view Butta's body.
They were dressed similarly in black Hugo Boss men's
suits. Under no circumstances would Dee put on a
dress. *Butta would understand.*

Brazen didn't question that.

It broke his heart to see shorty in a box. He felt
responsible. Maybe this was karma for all the loved ones he
had taken away from others.

Staring down into the mahogany coffin, Brazen
realized that Butta's head had been sewn back on crookedly.
It struck him that Butta seemed not to have a neck. Like
someone had just placed her head atop her shoulders

230

haphazardly and went about their business. This made Brazen bristle.

Silk is gonna pay for this!

Dee stared down at her boo. She leaned over into the casket and gently tried to straighten Butta's head. It was cold and stiff, and it would not move.

Dee's knees buckled.

Brazen put a hand on her elbow and held her up.

"I'm okay," she proclaimed after a minute or so.

Brazen let her go. They turned to go back to their seats. Dee's grief rose up like a tidal wave, she let out a loud guttural cry that caused Brazen to put his head down in his hands. The game was a cold-hearted bitch when it didn't go in your favor.

*****

Butta had been in the ground for a week. Dee had been in a hotel room drowning in her sorrow ever since. Empty bottles of assorted gin were everywhere, some shattered to pieces.

Shorty Got a Thug

Dee held her cell phone in her hand scrolling through pictures of her boo. Beautiful pictures of Butta that took Dee hard down memory lane.

Brazen's number kept popping up on the screen. Dee kept sending him to voicemail. She had been doing that for six days consecutively. Brazen kept hitting the REDIAL button, hoping Dee would eventually answer. After two dozen failed attempts to reach her by phone, he sent her a text: *Dee answer ya fkn phn!!!*

Still there was no reply.

If Dee would've answered her phone Brazen would have told her that it was time for them to get at Silk. Brazen had watched and followed the nigga for hours each of the past four days. He knew Silk's movements like he knew his own.

Several opportunities to hit Silk with an assault rifle, from a distance, had come and passed. Brazen didn't wanna pick off the nigga, he wanted to get close up on him. Snatch him up and serve him proper. But Silk kept himself surrounded by goons most of the time.

Brazen had a plan though.

Today he followed Silk's girl home from school. It had been easy to spot her in a crowd, she was rather tall with gold braids that hung down her back. She was Brazen's key to getting to Silk. But Brazen didn't wanna slump shorty along with her nigga. Something about her reminded Brazen of Ni. The two looked nothing alike, so maybe it was just that, like Ni, shorty's only mistake was that she loved a thug.

Dee finally decided to return Brazen's call.

"Where you at, shorty?" Brazen asked with concern.

"I'm where I'm at, man." Her voice was a bit slurred.

"Dee, quit playin'. Tell me where you're at. You sound like you been drinking."

"I have," she slurred.

"That's what's up. Tell me where you're at so I can come through and toss a few back with you," said Brazen. He could sense that she needed him.

"No, B, I wanna be alone," said Dee, looking down at the Desert Eagle in her hand.

She put the cell phone down on the night stand and put Brazen on loud speaker so that she could use her free hand to turn up the closest bottle of Seagrams. She took it straight to the head.

"Baby boy, we had a good little run. Nothing lasts forever. That's what life has taught me. Every day the deck gets reshuffled and the hand we get dealt is brand new. Sometimes we end up with no spades."

"I hear you and I agree with you, but we never throw our hand in—not muthafuckas like us. We go hard, Dee," Brazen pointed out.

"It's over, man. Don't you see that?"

"Nah, homegirl, it's never over. Not even when they toss dirt on our caskets. Then we haunt them bitch ass niggas in their sleep. C'mon, dawg, you're a G, don't talk like that."

Dee wept. She hated to let Brazen down but there was no more fight in her.

"Brazen, I loved her so much."

Her sobs hit Brazen hard. A tear fell from his eye without him realizing it. "I know you loved her. And Butta knew it too. Now we gotta get at the nigga who did that to her," insisted Brazen.

"I can't do it, B. Promise me you will. The game is over for me. It got the best of a bitch, I can't lie. It was all good when we were winning; when the

234

other side had to mourn theirs. But this shit right here…"

Dee couldn't even finish her thoughts. She slung the bottle of Seagram's gin against the wall. "I love you, Brazen. Get that nigga for me. I'm going wherever Butta went."

"No, shorty!" shouted Brazen.

Dee put the Desert Eagle to her head. She thought about the recoil, the way the powerful gun would jump when she pulled the trigger. It might misfire and not put her out. She could end up a vegetable.

She removed the gun from the side of her head and put it in her mouth.

"Dee! Talk to me, shorty! Say something!" Brazen's voice blared out of the phone.

The boom of the Desert Eagle sounded like a small cannon.

235

CHAPTER 55

Brazen's head hung and his shoulders slumped as he made it through the cemetery. The cold wind howled around him. He fought against the winter's cold by pulling his hoodie tighter around his face.

After just a few minutes of searching he found the marker that identified Dee's graveside. He had wanted to bury her next to her boo, but Butta's family wouldn't allow it.

It had taken more restraint than Brazen thought he had for him to calm the beast within him, and not crush Butta's entire fake ass family. Dee's resting place was way on the other side of the cemetery away from her love's—that was a crying shame.

Brazen hadn't attended Dee's funeral. He knew that Dee would understand; he had buried Tank and Butta, almost back to back. As strong as he was, Brazen just could not endure another funeral. Dee would know that there was no disrespect intended.

Brazen knelt at the small headstone and said a few private words to Dee. He could feel her presence around

236

him. The streets were saying that Dee had gone out bad, taking her own life. Brazen saw it much differently. "Shorty, I understand," he told her now. Her G wasn't diminished in his eyes. Contrary, the love that she had for Butta was elevated in Brazen's mind. Fuck whoever disagreed.

"I didn't come to talk about that though. I came to tell you that I'ma see about Silk. That's on my G! Rest in peace, shawdy. One," said Brazen, keeping it short and simple.

Nothing else to say, his gangsta would speak for itself. On behalf of his fallen soldiers.

*****

Silk had it going on. His new team was taking the game back to the 80's when crack first hit the ghettoNeither Silk nor any of his crew were old enough to have been around back in the day, but they had all heard the war stories. Now they were emulating drug crews from that era, making niggas *get down or lay down.*

Silk loved the rep he was building. He was gloating over the fact that he had almost single-handedly wiped out Brazen's entire squad. Like the real Rick Ross—not the rapper—Silk was a boss. *Brazen must've thought a nigga was gonna play the background forever.*

Silk pulled into his driveway. Two cars driven by his bodyguards pulled in behind him. They made sure that everything was good at Silk's house before leaving.

It was two o'clock in the morning and Silk was tired. He had been making moves for the past three days. He climbed the stairs up to his bedroom. Fatima was in bed asleep with the covers pulled up to her shoulders, only the back of her head faced the door. Her golden braids were wild tonight, Silk noted.

He removed his banger from his waist and set it down on the dresser. Stepping out of his jeans, Silk decided that a shower would have to wait until morning. He walked over to the bed in his boxers. Fatima didn't stir.

Silk turned off the bedside lamp and slid into bed, realizing that Fatima was on the side of the bed where he normally slept. "Shorty, you must be tired," he whispered.

The figure up under the covers quickly rolled over and jammed a Ruger in Silk's face. "It's Judgement Day muthafucka," grumbled Brazen.

Ca$h

Silk's mouth flew open in surprise, and then he tried to dart to the dresser where his gun lay. A bullet hit him in the spine before he could take two steps. Brazen turned on the lamp. The soft light and the braided golden wig made Brazen look demented.

Silk tried to crawl to his weapon but his spine had been severed by the gunshot and his legs would not do as his brain commanded.

With the toe of his Timbs, Brazen rolled Silk onto his back.

"You should've known that I was coming; that I would avenge La familia. You killed Tank and Butta as a way of taunting me. That was a mistake, real bosses know that you kill the head and the body will die," said Brazen.

He reached up under the bed and slid out the tennis bag that he had brought along. When he rose up he was holding a machete.

"You remember what you did to Butta?" He taunted his nemesis. "Yeah, nigga, I'm about to serve that shit right back at you the same way you dished it out.He carefully ran his finger down the razor sharp edge of the machete.

"Silk, I made a mistake by putting you on the team in the first place. But you made a bigger mistake by killing Butta and Tank and saving *me for last.*

Always go for the head first," said Brazen, raising the machete high above his head and bringing it down with force.

When bloody vengeance had been served, Brazen pulled the same ski mask over his face that he had worn when he creeped up behind Fatima and forced her in the house. He walked over to the closet where she was duct taped and gagged. He opened the closet door. Fatima was curled up in a ball.

"It's okay, Miss Lady, I'm not gonna hurt you. That's why I never allowed you to see my face. I want you to wait twenty minutes before you come out of this closet. If you come out any sooner I just might still be around. Do you understand me?" asked Brazen.

Fatima nodded 'yes'.

"I'm warning you that when you come out of this closet, you're gonna see the worse shit you've ever seen in your life. Let that be the reason you stay away from thugs."

With the bloody machete Brazen cut the binds from around her ankles.

"Take care and stay in school. I'll be watching," he said.

240

CHAPTER 56
EPILOGUE

Brazen pulled up to the address in Augusta, Georgia that Mrs. Smiley had given him. The GPS in his 2012 Maserati Kubang directed him to the proper house in this unfamiliar city.

Brazen put the SUV in park and killed the ignition. Trey Songz singing came to an abrupt halt. Brazen made sure that the doors were locked after getting out of the Maserati. Although it appeared to be a nice neighborhood, Brazen wasn't taking any chances, those duffel bags and the safe in the back of the SUV contained money that had cost him almost everyone he loved.

He checked himself over in the side mirror and was pleased with his new swag. Gone were the jeans, Timbs, and hoodies. Brazen was rocking black wool Hugo Boss slacks, a black Hugo Boss sweater, Gators on his feet, and a black fur jacket. His waves were still spinning in his head, and they tapered down into neatly trimmed sideburns that blended down into a newly grown goatee. He was definitely getting his grown man on.

In his arms he carried a large bouquet of pink roses. Inside the pocket of his fur jacket was a better surprise. He walked up on the porch and rang the doorbell.

Niesha answered the door wearing a look of indifference. "Hi, Brazen," She spoke and let him in. "Mama told me to expect you."

Brazen looked at Niesha with his mouth wide open. Her belly was poking way out!

"What happened to you?" he asked.

"This," Ni replied, grabbing his crotch. "Don't act like you don't remember. And you can stop acting surprised because you're not doing nothing but acting. Mama already told me that she spilled the beans."

Brazen couldn't help but laugh. *Mrs. Smiley can't hold water!*

"You look beautiful, shorty. You got that glow that people be talking about with pregnant women. So this is why you left?"

"Yes, I had to protect this little life that's inside of me." She smiled, placing both hands on her stomach.

"Well, I don't blame you, but I missed you like hell. I mean, damn, a nigga was sick."

"I was sick without you, too. Please tell me that you're really out of the game." She needed to hear him say it.

"I'm done, baby girl," he said with sincerity. He handed her the pink roses. "I love you, Ni."

"So you say," she teased.

She sat the roses down on the end table, stood on her tippy toes and gave him a kiss. "I love you too."

Brazen held her hands in his. He told her about the house on Miami Beach and the riches outside in the Maserati.

"Wow! That's a lot of money, Brazen," gasped Niesha.

"Let me go outside and bring it in so you can see what it looks like," he offered.

"You can show me later. Besides, the money isn't important, I'm just happy to have you. Now come and let me show *you* something." Niesha said.

She pulled him along by the hand.

Following her upstairs Brazen asked, "What you got to show me?"

"You'll see," she replied, smiling at him over her shoulder.

Shorty Got a Thug

Brazen stopped her, turned her where she would be facing him; took her hand in his and he went down on bended knee. Niesha almost lost her breath when she saw what he pulled out of the pocket of his fur jacket.

Brazen opened the small black velvet box and extracted the most beautiful diamond engagement ring Niesha had ever seen. And the diamond was huge! She didn't care how many carats it was, it could have come out of a bubble gum machine and her smile would have been just as wide. Her heart would have been beating just as fast.

"Ni, I love you. Will you—"

"Yes! Yes! Yes!" Ni screamed, and they both laughed at her impatience.

Brazen rose to his feet and they kissed passionately. He held her in his arms and said, "Dark Cream, I'm sorry for all that I put you through. If I could go back and change things..."

Niesha was only half listening; she was too busy pulling him upstairs.

"What's up shorty?" asked Brazen.

"Boy, don't play. I'm going to need you to feed your baby," smirked Niesha.

Ca$h

Brazen smiled and swooped her up in his arms and carried her the rest of the way up the stairs. She wrapped her arms around his neck and closed her eyes as anticipation caused her heart to flutter like they were about to make love for the very first time.

By the time they made it to the bedroom and Brazen laid her down on the bed, Niesha's pussy was throbbing. "Hurry baby," she rushed him.

And when Brazen undressed her, then himself, and slowly entered her slippery wet paradise, Niesha cried out his name and thanked God for finally allowing her love for him to be rewarded.

-THE END-

Shorty Got a Thug

Also check out my other titles:

Books Under Wahida Clark Publishing

TRUST NO MAN

TRUST NO MAN 2 (Disloyalty is Unforgivable)

TRSUT NO MAN 3 (Life Father, Like Son)

BONDED BY BLOOD

Independently Released Titles

SHORTY GOT A THUG

THUGS CRY

THUGS CRY 2

A DIRTY SOUTH LOVE w/Jennifer Luckett

TRUST NO BITCH w/Nene Capri

TRUST NO BITCH 2: Deadly Silence w/Nene

Capri

Ca$h

INTERVIEW WITH CA$H

Q: What inspired you to start writing? And how were you able to become a force in street lit from behind bars?

A: I've always been a writer at heart but I was too caught up in the game to pursue writing when I was on the streets. As soon as I came to prison I picked up my pen. Of course this was the early 90's way before there was a true vehicle to get these type of stories published. Once I read The Coldest Winter Ever, then *True to the Game* and *B-More Careful* I was determined to get my work published. Eventually I self-published. My self-published novel attracted the attention of the Queen herself, Mrs. Wahida Clark, and the rest is history.

Q: Are you still signed to Wahida Clark Presents Publishing?

247

A: Nah I have my own publishing company now Lock Down Publications.

Q: Okay. How long have you been incarcerated?

A: I'm on my 22nd year. Hopefully I'll get out in 2014, but you never know, it's insane behind these walls.

Q: How do you come up with the concepts and characters for your novels?

A: It's simple, I write about what I know. Enough said.

Q: In *Shorty Got a Thug,* the characters Brazen and Niesha, were they people you know forreal?

A: There's a Niesha and Brazen is every city all over the nation. That's why my readers can relate to the shit I write. Because although it's fiction, it's not make believe. Sometimes I change the names to protect the guilty.

Q: What other titles do you have out?

Ca$h

A: I have four titles out on the Wahida Clark Presents imprint. *Trust No Man, Trust no Man 2(Disloyalty is Unforgivable) Trust No Man 3, and Bonded by Blood.* And 6 under Lock Down. Thugs Cry 1&2, Trust No Bitch 1&2, A Dirty South Love, and Shorty Got A Thug.

Q: Who are some of your favorite authors?

A: Wahida Clark, of course, and everything WCP, especially Anthony Fields(The Ultimate Sacrifice), Mike Sanders (Thirsty 1&2), and this new sistah named NeNe Capri(The Pussy Trap), she's sick with her pen. Al Saadiq Banks, Dutch, my homie Cole Hart, Karen Williams, and Ashley & JaQuavis half of the time (laughs).Then there's three ladies who move in silence, doing their own thing— , La'Tonya West and Aleta Williams. Neither is a household name in the industry yet, but I've watched them grow as writers and remain ambitious in the face of adversity. So it's all love for these ambitious ladies.

Q: What is it like being on lock for more than two decades? I can't even imagine that.

A: No, you can't, so I won't try to explain it.

Q: Well, you seem to be handling it well.

A: That's because I'm trained to go. Prison can't bring nothing out of you that's not inside you. I was a solid dude when I came in, and that's how I'll leave, whether I walk out of these gates one day or get carried out.

Q: Is there anything you would like to say to your readers?

A: Of course, I would like to thank them for supporting what I do. Without them my voice would be trapped behind prison walls along with my body. When you purchase and read my books it's very important to me for you to go to Amazon.com or Goodreads or wherever and post a review. It's my only way to know what you think of my stories. A book is not a success because someone buys it. What makes it a success is when the person who read it tells others about it.

On another note, it's my duty as a triple OG to warn the young impressionable dudes out there who might come across my books, there are no winners in the life that I write about. Even when a dude make it out of the game as Brazen did in *Shorty Got a Thug*, he leaves behind a trail of destruction. And he carries forward a guilt so thick it's hard to breathe.

Most times, in real life, the "Brazens" end up dead or in prison, which for all intents and purposes is one and the same. Because prison is death too, it's just dying one day at a time. If I could, I would write a tragic ending to every story I write, because that's reality. For the sake of entertainment and suspense I can't do that. But don't be fooled, the game spares NO ONE.

Q: That's deep. Anything else you want to say?

A: Never give up. Peace.

CPSIA information can be obtained at www.ICGtesting.com
Printed in the USA
LVOW08s1411110214

373254LV00001B/25/P